Three-Way

Three-Way

EROTIC STORIES

EDITED BY

ALISON TYLER

CLEIS
PRESS

Published in the United States by Cleis Press Inc., P.O. Box 14684, San Francisco, California 94114.

Printed in the United States.
Cover design: Scott Idleman

Text design: Frank Wiedemann
Cleis logo art: Juana Alicia
First Edition.
10 9 8 7 6 5 4 3 2

"Share" by M. Christian, "The New Fiancée" by N. T. Morley, and "In Town for Business" by Zach Addams appeared at www.goodvibes.com. An earlier version of "Nine Ball, Corner Pocket" by Michelle Houston appeared at www.threepillows.com. "1-900-FANTASY" by Dante Davidson appeared in *Bondage on a Budget* (Masquerade, 1997). "If You Can Make It There, You Can Make It Anywhere" by A. J. Stone appeared in *Best Lesbian Erotica 2001* (Cleis Press, 2000). "Cast of Three" by Emilie Paris appeared in *Sweet Life* (Cleis Press, 2001). "Pink Elephants" by Eric Williams appeared in *Naughty Stories from A to Z, Volume 3* (Pretty Things Press, 2004). "The Space Between" by Helena Settimana appeared at www.erotica-readers.com.

For SAM

Acknowledgements

To my constant support team: Violet Blue, Eliza Castle,
Mike Ostrowski, Barbara Pizio, Thomas S. Roche,
Alex Mendra, Kerri Sharp, and, of course,
Felice Newman and Frédérique Delacoste

"I believe that sex is a beautiful thing between two people.
Between five, it's fantastic."
—Woody Allen

Contents

Introduction

I had my first threesome when I was nineteen.

Ah, you can just see me, can't you? You imagine a worldly, smoldering vixen, so clever that she actually managed to choreograph a ménage à trois before she could even legally drink.

Not the case, of course.

Actually, I had my first taste of a threesome when I was eighteen. But according to *Playboy*, if it's two guys and one girl, the correct term is "gangbang." Also not the case, of course.

My first tentative tango with more than one partner came before I'd even been one on one. I went out with two close guy friends to an off-campus apartment and we wiled away the night drinking tequila and telling dirty fantasies. At some point, I found myself sandwiched naked between my two buddies, and we slept together like that, all night long. No sex, okay, but excitement that was undeniable. Excitement that left me craving more. Because that's what ménages à trois are all about: MORE.

At nineteen, I was ready for the sex. My sultry blonde editor, Ava, invited me to her house on a stormy night, during which she and her handsome male roommate enlightened me on many of the things three people could do in one bed during a blackout.

Since then, I've never looked back. Why should I? Three means more of everything. Maybe I'm greedy, but when it comes to sex, I like more. More fingers. More tongues. More limbs. More tangling and wrestling on the mattress. Here are snapshots of my first real threesome: Ava and me taking turns sucking Josh's rock-hard cock; me licking Ava's breasts while Josh fucked her; Ava telling Josh exactly how to go down on me—and, oh, was she experienced; candlelight flickering over our naked bodies; limbs entwined like something out of a sleekly seductive porn film.

More than a decade later, I still remember exactly what I was wearing that night: gossamer-light skirt, silky peach panties, black top, huge silver hoop earrings. I know the subtle scent of my perfume, the deep red of my lipstick, and how I looked the morning after when I went to the local grocery store to get coffee. My friend Kelly worked there. He was my on-and-off-again fuckbuddy, and he sidled up to me like a panther, seeming to tell from my scent that something had changed.

"What are you doing?"

"Caffeine injection," I smiled sleepily at him.

"But you look different. Where were you last night?"

"With Ava…"

"And?" he pressed.

"Josh…"

I learned from the look on his face how turned-on guys get by the thought. That evening won me mileage for months with Kelly, gave me such an upper hand that I was giddy with delight from the heights. I still am, to tell the truth. Who did I think I was, playing around with these older and much more knowledgeable playmates? Who do I think I am now, juggling threesomes and foursomes like some perverted acrobat in Cirque du Soleil?

I guess I'm just someone who always wants a little bit more....

But luckily for us all I'm not the only one—because the authors in this collection follow the same school of thought. From Thomas S. Roche's sizzling "Two Guys and a Girl," to Dante Davidson's steamy "1-900-FANTASY," the stories in this collection are among my all-time favorites. I've chosen pieces that are classic threeways, as well as more unusual ménages à trois, such as creative genius Tom Piccirilli's "Craving Faces," which features a threeway between a man, a woman, and the woman's tattooed alter ego. (Prepare to be impressed.)

In "Third Party," Dawn M. Pares focuses on the rules for a three-course situation, while Marilyn Jaye Lewis reminisces on a threeway from long ago in the deliciously naughty "Three for the Money." Several pieces feature slippery orgies, such as "Circle of Friends" by Rebecca Henderson, but all have one thing in common: they prove that three (or four or five) is definitely the charm!

Alison Tyler
July 2004
San Francisco

Share

M. Christian

Favorite thing: hot and hot and hotter, sitting there and other places. Two playmates, lovers, pals; in bedrooms, hot tubs, at parties (where everyone else is doing the same or more or less all around). Let's do this, I say: Let's do something hotter than fucking, let's do this—hotter than sucking. People fuck and suck for others, often. Folks do what they do with and for each other when they fuck and suck: they step up on stage and bow to the audience and expect applause when they're finished. Now, I say, let's do something dark and loaded and nasty. Something you don't do for someone else. Something you do for yourself. Share this, I say, share this and I'll share what I do for myself. Let's do something private, in public: for me and for you.

Ever seen a man masturbate? Would you like to? Would you like to touch me while I stroke my cock, pull on my balls and watch and touch you? Would you like to see me take a bit of lube on my hand and slowly stroke myself till I'm hard, hard, hard? See my cock, so hard and smooth. I like my cock: I like the way it feels when I stroke it. I like the smoothness of the skin, the firmness of the shaft. I like my cut head, the way it feels when I go from base to ridge to tip. My cock doesn't have a pet name; he doesn't lead me around because he is me. "He" is a part of me that responds when I get excited, when I excite myself. Do you want to do something? What do you like to do when you get excited? What do you want to do when you see me doing this—stroking my cock, looking at your lovely body, all rosy and warm, all hot and sticky and hard in all the right places? Please, feel free to touch yourself. Show me as I show you: you are hot and I have to touch myself. Are you hot? Please, touch yourself.

At home with my sexy wife, at hot tubs and in other bedrooms with my playmates and friends, at parties with more playmates and friends and maybe strangers whose names I'll never know. Share and share alike. You are lovely, I say/mean, as their fingers stroke and fondle, as their eyes glaze but never leave mine and my straight and tensed body, my straight and firm cock. You are so sexy, I say, kissing, touching with other hands. Sitting, maybe standing next to each other in the heat of our bodies, letting our skins dance against each other, bathing in our sweat and steam. I love to do this as you do this, I say, and lick and fondle their nipples, arms, chests, breasts, backs. So hot, I mumble, so hot, so hot—putting my hand on theirs, not on them, not there directly, but just hand on hand—to feel, to be there for them as they rub and stroke and pull and twist. I lie there next to them, hands on hands on the spot of their excitement, lying there with them as they bring, and I bring, ourselves up and over.

So...nice, such a special sharing. We have the best that we can have; the best that we can share of something that is really ourselves; something we can do so, so, so well because who knows us better?

Share and share alike, together.

Three for the Money

MARILYN JAYE LEWIS

Yesterday, I went to a funeral uptown. When I left my apartment in the morning, it had been the proverbial spring day, birds chirping, daffodils blooming in the park—the works. Naturally, by the time I came up from the subway station an hour and a half later, it had begun to rain. Funerals are a bit like rain dances in that way; people gather together in mourning, and the earth itself cries.

The dead guy, Marten Santos, had been notoriously rich and depraved while he was alive. He had never tried to pass as righteous, though, never pretended to be perfect. We all knew about his peculiar tastes and erratic passions, and loved him for that. Nevertheless, he'd been raised a strict Roman Catholic and so the funeral was a stuffy, conservative affair, held at Our Lady of Divine Sorrows. After the funeral, as the teary-eyed pallbearers removed the casket from the church and solemnly loaded it into the back of the hearse, Our Lady's bell tolled mournfully, sounding all the more poignant in the gray drizzle of rain. He was a man who was going to be missed by a lot of good people.

In life, Mr. Santos had been one of my favorite tricks. When he died suddenly of a heart attack three days ago, the newspaper said that he was pushing seventy. During the year when he'd been one of my regulars, he claimed to be fifty-five. It says a lot that after all these years I was moved enough by a sense of loss to attend his funeral. But then, he hadn't always been a trick. With Mr. Santos, I'd done the unthinkable and allowed a favorite john to become a lover, or nearly so. The shame of that slipup on my part, and a difficult scene he put me through in a cheap hotel room, had caused us to part on uncomfortable terms. Still, it made me no less fond of him.

I don't turn tricks anymore, I haven't for years. I'm almost forty now. I work in a respectable office and I earn a respectable living. I present a very hard-assed, successful-bitch version of myself to the world and it's helped me to succeed and keep my past where it should be, in the past. The frantic, frenetic survival skills acquired by all New Yorkers makes the town a forgiving place. As long as you don't wind up at the heart of a sordid public scandal in a court of law, where New Yorkers show their ugly sides and revel in seeing your past mistakes slung at you like so much mud, you can do just about anything to get ahead in this town and not have to worry too much that it'll come back to haunt you.

Mr. Santos and I first met in an upscale espresso shop on the Upper East Side. This was back in the '80s, when a whole lot of people had money to burn. Mr. Santos was friends with the owner, Hajid, who was one of my regulars, too. Hajid liked getting blow jobs behind the desk in his office. His office was in the basement of the coffee house. It was decidedly downscale in that dark, damp, vermin-infested cellar. However, a simple blow job, as long as I was willing to have my pants around my knees and keep my naked ass out for his viewing pleasure, lasted only about ten minutes and garnered me two hundred tax-free dollars, so I found ways to make even that *ratskeller* seem erotic.

The evening I met Mr. Santos, I was actually just having coffee. I wasn't engaged in business. Hajid and I were on friendly terms. He introduced me to Mr. Santos, with a nod and a wink, and Mr. Santos pulled up a chair. He got right down to the business of getting to know me better. He ended the meeting by paying my modest tab and then asking me for my phone number, which of course I gave him since it was obvious he was loaded—even more so than Hajid.

Our trysts started out simple and straightforward. Mr. Santos would always arrange for me to meet him in other rich people's high-class apartments. The people he knew went on extended vacations, traveled on business to faraway places, or had primary homes in other countries. Mr. Santos was married back then, and apparently he and his other married male friends formed a cozy circle of infidels, each leaving the rest of the crew a key to his empty apartment for extramarital liaisons in his absence. I don't think the wives ever had a clue what was taking place in the sanctity of their homes while they were off on holiday.

I was never to touch anything, never allowed to get too comfortable in the jaw-dropping luxury of our trysting places.

Mr. Santos liked anal and that was pretty much the sole basis of our get-togethers, at first. Without fanfare, he would unzip his trousers; let them fall unceremoniously to his ankles, along with his boxers. He'd slip on a rubber; slather it with the lube that he carried in his pocket in handy individual foil packets. Then I'd bend over anything steady and he'd slide his cock up my ass.

He fucked me like a man who had important meetings to get to, so he usually came pretty quickly. I didn't have to say anything weird, or dress in anything unusual. I simply had to show up with an absolutely clean asshole, bend over and let him ream me; that was all he required. For that, I got five hundred dollars cash; five crisp, one-hundred-dollar bills, folded in the middle, which he'd place under my nose while I was still bending over—before he'd even pulled his cock out of me, I'd get paid.

There was something about the way he paid me that tended to make me feel a little humiliated, but he didn't seem to think twice about it. By the time I'd turn around, he'd have the used condom off, his trousers pulled up, and would be heading to the toilet to flush the condom down. He never said anything like, "Here's your money, you whore," or "Take that, bitch." He just had a funny habit of leaving it parked under my nose while my ass was still stuffed with him.

I remember when we had our first real conversation. It was a day when he seemed to be at leisure. He wasn't pressed for time, wasn't hurrying. It was a day when he wandered around the spacious apartment we were using, looking for the perfect place to bend me over, making small talk, making jokes. "Bend over that chair there, let me see the view. Pull up your skirt. No, we can find something better."

When he finally decided on the perfect spot—an ergonomically correct artist's stool—he lifted my skirt himself, pulled my panties down (an intimate gesture he'd never once done before) and then said, "You know what this reminds me of?"

My naked ass in the air, my thighs spread in anticipation, my head hanging down, I said, "No, what?"

"Church. This reminds me of church."

He didn't elaborate and I had no idea what he was talking about. But the thought of church seemed to make him feel even more jovial. He sank to his knees and rimmed me, his hot, wet tongue expertly stroking my puckered hole. It felt sensational. I actually moaned and felt like touching myself.

Having his nose in my ass seemed to arouse his passion, for that day he fucked my ass especially vigorously, nearly knocking me off the stool several times. The mounting pressure of his thickening hard-on sucking in and out of my ass made me cry out. When he came, he pulled his cock out a little aggressively, gave me a resounding smack on my upturned ass, and said, "Here you go. Thanks, kiddo." And the money was once again placed in front of my face—on this occasion, I'd been staring at a parquet floor.

His breezy pre-sex conversing, combined with his sudden rugged manner with me during sex, made me see Mr. Santos in a different light. He was a handsome man, I decided, as I watched him zip up his trousers and go off in search of the toilet. I still had my panties around my knees when he came back into the room. I was lingering in my little swoon.

"What's with you?" he asked.

Snapping out of it and feeling embarrassed, I moved to

pull up my panties.

"No, wait." He stopped me. "Not yet. You feel like making a little extra money today?"

I was caught off guard. He fished out his wallet and surveyed its contents. "Well, I have ten whole dollars." He found this amusing. "What do you feel like doing for ten dollars?"

"What did you have in mind?"

"I want to try something and see if I can make you come."

I never, under any circumstances, came with a trick. But Mr. Santos intrigued me. "You think you can make me come for ten dollars?"

"Ten bucks, and a nice dinner. What do you say to that? My wife's out of town and I've got all the time in the world. I'll make it up to you next time about the money. You know I'm good for it."

I was feeling game. I liked Mr. Santos. I wasn't worried about the money.

He told me to step out of my panties completely, then to squat down on the parquet floor. He told me that under no circumstances should I touch myself; he wanted to do all the work. He lubed two of his fingers, squatted down next to me, held me around my shoulders to sort of brace me, and then he stuck the two lubed fingers up my ass. He wiggled them vigorously in there, pushing hard against my perineum, rubbing the wall of muscle with all his strength.

"*Oh god,*" I squealed in sheer ecstasy, clutching him tight, a stream of piss suddenly squirting out of me and forming a puddle on the nice wood floor.

"Go for it, baby. Let everything go. We can clean this up later. Bear down on me."

I did as he suggested, pushing my asshole down around his hardworking fingers, never dreaming that I could be launched into orgasm like a rocket without direct pressure applied to my clit. But it happened. My thighs shook as I squatted and bore down, more fluids gushing out of my open pisshole. My body was overwhelmed by waves of pleasure as his fingers rubbed more vigorously against the pressure of my now frantically contracting sphincter.

When I was through hyperventilating and convulsing like a lunatic, Mr. Santos was still holding me, smiling. "Did you come?" he asked, very pleased with himself.

I didn't take the extra ten dollars that day, but I took him up on his offer to buy me dinner and that was the beginning of a new chapter in our 'business relationship.'

He continued to pay me whenever we got together, but we talked more, he took more time with me, he felt challenged to give me orgasms in unexpected ways. Soon, he was paying for rooms in five-star hotels, where we'd disappear for entire days together, relying on room service for sustenance. He introduced blindfolds, light bondage, and spanking to the list of things we were now doing with each other regularly in a lavish king-sized bed.

"Do you ever eat pussy?" he asked me one afternoon. "I mean, do you ever get asked to do that when you're out on a call?"

I looked at him uneasily, not at all pleased that the world of my other tricks was even remotely entering into our time together.

"Do you even know *how* to eat pussy?"

"Of course I do."

"You get paid to do that?"

"Sometimes." I didn't feel much like discussing it.

"I'd like to see you eat pussy, you know that?"

You and every other trick on earth, I told myself. The last thing I wanted was to bring another girl into our scene, a girl who might prove to be more novel than me, a girl who might walk off with his number in her purse and then I would lose my favorite trick. Mr. Santos was now the man I fantasized about when I was home alone in bed. I didn't think he would leave his wife for me, or anything like that, but I naively considered us lovers. I'd begun to hate the fact that he still paid me.

"What's that face for?" he said. "You aren't into pussy?"

"Girls are all right."

"I was thinking more along the lines of a woman—not a girl."

He immediately piqued my interest. "You mean you have someone in mind?"

"To be honest, there's a woman I've been seeing off and on for years, since before I was married. Occasionally, we get together when our spouses are otherwise detained and we have sex. I told her about you. How much fun you are. How amenable you can be."

And whose idea was it to make it a threesome, I wondered suspiciously, hers, or his?

"She'll pay you the same amount I do; you'll get double your usual fee. It wouldn't be a question of taking advantage. I would really like to see you eat her pussy. And I think she has an idea of a scene of her own. She's very willing to pay you," he repeated. "I don't think she's ever paid anyone to do a scene with her. Or to have *any* kind of sex with her, for that matter.

She's just a regular married woman, but a good friend of mine."

She sounded harmless enough. But you'd think after my years of turning tricks, I would have known beyond a doubt that people who sound harmless can be the most difficult customers when it's all said and done.

Still, I agreed to do the three-way. We made an appointment for an afternoon the following week. For some reason, we were meeting in a tacky hotel in midtown—gone was the luxury of the king-sized bed, the crisp white sheets and room service. Everything about the hotel they'd chosen was dingy, seedy, and low class.

Mr. Santos had asked me to bring along an outfit that would be suitable for a naughty little girl routine. Even though I'd never gone to Catholic school myself, I had a vintage Catholic schoolgirl uniform that fit me perfectly. I figured Mr. Santos would get off on the religion thing so that's what I packed for my change of clothes.

I'd been getting steadily more into the idea of the three-way as the day approached. Anything that involved the unpredictability of Mr. Santos's lusty libido aroused my own sexual appetites. He was nothing like an average trick. So when I knocked on the hotel room door that afternoon, I was already horny, already sopping wet between my legs. Until Mr. Santos let me into the room and introduced me to his woman friend.

Oh my god, I realized in sick horror, *it's Mrs. Hamilton.*

She'd been my tenth grade sociology teacher. A woman who'd made my life a living hell for an entire year. I was certain it was her. To this day, I don't know if she recognized me, too. If she did, she never once let on. But I *knew* it was her. She was simply using a fake name, like a lot of tricks do.

"Call me either 'Daddy' or 'Sir' today," Mr. Santos was instructing me. "And this is your new stepmother, Louise."

Louise? They couldn't come up with anything less corny than Louise?

I had that feeling of panic in my gut that I used to get in my early days of hustling; I wanted to bolt. But then I focused on the money: one thousand dollars cash for a single afternoon's work. It would be worth it. But I saw immediately that it was going to be just that—work.

Mrs. Hamilton had never been an unattractive woman; it was just that she'd always been a mean bitch of a teacher. In my years since high school, she'd managed to stay attractive; she'd taken good care of herself. I figured that if she knew Mr. Santos, she must have money, too, and that always helps women stay good-looking. Yet it made me wonder why she'd chosen to teach at all. Perhaps for the sick thrill of tormenting teenagers?

"Louise wants to help you change clothes," Mr. Santos told me. "It'll give you two a chance to get comfortable with each other. I'm going to run across the street to the liquor store. This trashy hotel doesn't even supply booze."

Shit. He was leaving me alone with her. The dreaded moment was starting to look even worse. Not only would I have to get naked for Mrs. Hamilton, I would have to be completely alone with her while it happened. No horny Mr. Santos around to use as a buffer zone.

When he was gone, she went right into 'efficient teacher' mode. "Come here," she said flatly. "Let's get you out of those clothes and into something more appropriate."

She didn't act like it made her at all nervous to be around a prostitute, to be doing a scene. I wondered if she was anybody's horny lesbo stepmother in real life. The implications of that thought creeped me out. I had to force myself to keep my mind a blank.

Mrs. Hamilton was going through my bag, pulling out my change of clothes. She seemed to recognize the uniform for what it was—something *real* girls wore in *real* high schools. "Are you Catholic?" she asked. "Not that it's any of my business."

"Yes," I said. "But I went to *public* schools." The sudden rudeness in my tone surprised even me.

She eyed me coolly, taking in that last remark. "Come over here," she said.

Shit. She was actually making me nervous. But I went over to her. Without hesitating, she began undressing me. "Let me tell you something," she explained carefully, unbuttoning my shirt with manicured fingers. "While we're in the confines of this room, while we're on the clock, so to speak, I have no qualms whatsoever about making it very clear which one of us is on top." The sound of her words alone felt like a slap. She had my shirt off. She was moving to unfasten my bra then, her fingers were touching the skin on my back, her face was close to mine. I didn't like it. "If you want to keep talking to me in that rude tone," she continued, "go right ahead. But consider yourself warned. I'm not afraid of girls like you. I deal with your kind every day."

My bra was off. My tits were right there in front of her, my nipples shivering to stiff points from the sudden change in temperature. How many times had I bared my tits for strange clients? But this took the cake for strangeness. I felt exposed.

She didn't touch me, though. She barely even paused to look at my nakedness. She was already on to my tight jeans, unzipping them, tugging them down to my ankles.

I was in that state of half-undressed nervousness when Mr. Santos came back to the room, carrying a fifth of gin and a large carton of Tropicana OJ.

Jesus, I wondered, *how trashy are we going to get?* Where was the top-shelf bourbon, or at the very least, some cheap champagne?

"Well," he said, regarding us with satisfaction, "we're certainly progressing here. Anyone want a drink?"

We all did. Mr. Santos played bartender while keeping a keen eye on us.

Mrs. Hamilton had me completely undressed, except for my panties. Those she seemed to want to take more time with. She lowered them slowly, anticipating the unveiling of my neatly trimmed snatch. She was actually squatting down in front of me, apparently wanting an up close and personal view. It made me even more uncomfortable—not so much that Mrs. Hamilton was squatting down in front of me, so obviously aroused by the imminent sight of another woman's pussy, but the fact that I was getting off on it, too. I was suddenly wet again.

"*Good lord,*" she said quickly under her breath. She'd peeled my panties past my mound, rolled them partially down my thighs and seen the strand of gooey wetness connecting my soaking hole to the cotton crotch of my underwear. She looked up at Mr. Santos, who was now standing next to us, offers of drinks in his hands. "She's so wet," Mrs. Hamilton explained in quiet earnestness, as if the sight of a twat swollen in arousal pained her deliciously.

I took my drink from Mr. Santos and gulped it down. I needed fortification. Mrs. Hamilton was fucking *hot.* And now she was licking me, her mouth was actually on me down there, and I was getting off on it.

Jesus, I wondered; what was going to happen here? Alone, unsupervised with two horny tricks who could get me this worked up; two people apparently intent on doing a pseudo-incest scene, with me playing the part of the helpless bottom; two tops wanting to have their way with me, and all of us downing cheap gin?

I was light-headed. I parted my legs as much as I could for Mrs. Hamilton, but it wasn't easy with my panties around my thighs. She held tight to my asscheeks, her mouth flush with my mound. She moaned as her hot tongue slid eagerly around in the folds of my pussy lips, occasionally landing directly on the tip of my clit. I was soon so aroused by the lusty sounds she made, that I actually held on to her head to keep myself steady. I had a handful of Mrs. Hamilton's hair in one hand, and a plastic cup of gin and OJ in the other. It all seemed so decadently tawdry. The cheap thrill of it made me press Mrs. Hamilton's face even closer to my snatch, rubbing her face in the slippery folds of it. The horny bitch moaned even more.

Mr. Santos lit a cigarette. He stood close to us, watching it all unfold, feeling up my titties while he watched—taking firm handfuls of titty flesh and squeezing, kneading, then tugging roughly on my stiff, aching nipples. He took a drag off his cigarette and then put his mouth on mine, forcing his exhaled smoke into my open mouth along with his tongue.

The feel of his tongue filling my mouth, and Mrs. Hamilton's tongue deep between my sopping lips, while Mr. Santos kept up his avid mauling of my breasts—I thought I'd come right on the spot.

But Mr. Santos had his thoughts elsewhere. He pulled away from me the second before I had a chance to come. "This is going to be good," he announced.

The sound of his voice seemed to bring Mrs. Hamilton back to earth. She got up from between my legs abruptly, her mouth a slick mess. She went straight for the drink awaiting her on the dresser. I could see her mentally pulling herself together; reminding *herself* which one of us girls was on top.

Within moments, she was in stepmother mode. "I want you to go into the bathroom and put on your clothes. Your father and I want to be alone. We'll tell you when to come out."

I did as I was told, stopping first to refresh my drink. I closed myself up in the small, ugly bathroom and got into my uniform. Outside, I could hear the lusty sounds of them going at each other. I didn't know in what way. Had they managed to strip out of their clothes in record time and begin fucking? Were they only partially undressed and sucking each other, or—just what were they doing? I was not only keenly curious, I was also jealous. I didn't want Mr. Santos to enjoy Mrs. Hamilton *that* much; after all, he was *my* lover.

Of course, I'd been instructed to stay put in the bathroom until I was given permission to come out. But that was all part of the scene. Naughty girls went wide-eyed into every opportunity to misbehave. Otherwise, you'd deprive your scene-mates of the chance to spank you bare-assed—or worse, depending on the infraction.

I quietly cracked open the bathroom door and peeked out at them.

I'll be damned, I thought.

They were fucking, all right. But they were, for the most

part, still dressed. Mrs. Hamilton was bent over the foot of the bed with her pants tugged down to her knees, while Mr. Santos, cock out of his unzipped trousers, rode her hard from behind.

I was transfixed—they were in such a frenzy of lust. Plus the cheap booze had gone to my head. I couldn't believe I was watching Mrs. Hamilton get nailed, and in such an unflattering posture. Her white ass looked huge, sticking out like that.

I worked my hand up under my skirt and inside my white panties. I wiggled my clit furiously as I watched them fuck like dogs.

As if on cue, Mrs. Hamilton glanced over at the bathroom door and caught me spying on them. It seemed to make her ass jut out even more, if that was possible. But she got a queer look on her face, too, like she couldn't wait to get down and nasty on my own ass. I quickly closed the bathroom door and tried to mind my own business.

Naturally it was too late, and the incest-punishment scene was in full swing. There was soon a knock on the bathroom door. When I opened it, it was "Daddy." He said, "Your stepmother wishes to speak to you."

I came out of the bathroom to find my "stepmother" stark naked, sitting on the bed. She looked good naked, but she looked angry. "Come over here," she said.

I expected to get thoroughly spanked by her and I wasn't sure whether or not I would get off on it; she was still Mrs. Hamilton after all, a woman I had once despised. As I went to her, there was a fear in my belly reminiscent of what I had once felt facing actual punishment as a child. Of course, this wasn't a scene remotely close to anything that would have gone on in my own house. I hadn't lost sight of the fact that we were all here for sex.

Daddy, still fully clothed, only his cock jutting out from his pants, sat down on the bed next to the naked "Louise." He had a stern expression on his face that made him look even more handsome. I was hoping he would force me to make it up to him somehow—all his disappointment in how I had misbehaved. But for now, the emphasis was on Louise. This was decidedly her scene, the part she was paying for.

"Come closer," she said.

I stood directly in front of her, cowering in my schoolgirl uniform.

"What were you doing in there?" she demanded.

"Nothing."

"It was more than nothing, young lady. You were spying on us, weren't you?"

"Yes," I meekly confessed.

"Weren't you told to stay in there until someone came for you?"

"Yes."

"And why did you disobey me?"

"I don't know."

"I'll tell you why, because you're a dirty little girl, aren't you? What do you suppose happens to a dirty little girl who disobeys and sticks her nose where it doesn't belong?"

I gave it some serious thought. The look in Mrs. Hamilton's eyes was dark and unpleasant. Mr. Santos, however, was in the throes of lust. He was watching it all while avidly stroking himself.

"I asked you a question," my stepmother went on. "What

do you suppose happens to a dirty little girl who disobeys?"

"I don't know," I replied.

"I think you do."

I said nothing.

"Answer me."

"I guess I need to get spanked!" I finally blurted.

I was playing my part to the hilt now and Mrs. Hamilton had succumbed completely to the erotic pull of her role. She was so obviously entranced by the power of her anger. "That's right. You need a good spanking to teach you a lesson. Get over here, right over my knee, young lady."

She grabbed me and pulled me over her knee, positioning me across her lap in such a way that everything between my legs would be facing Mr. Santos. She lifted my skirt. "I'll teach you to be a dirty little girl," she said, lowering my panties with deliberate patience, slowly revealing the round, white globes of my ass, then tugging the panties down my thighs.

She held my wrists tight and then gave my ass a resounding spank. "Why do you dirty girls always have to learn the hardest way how to behave?" She gave me another well-placed, stinging spank.

"I want you to tell Daddy exactly what you did; tell him why I'm so angry with you." Another severe smack heated my cheeks, making me jump.

"Because I was watching," I cried out.

"Watching what?" The smacks were coming more quickly now, stinging, landing relentlessly on the same spot. My ass burned. I tried to wriggle away from the aim of her blows, but it was to no avail. "Answer me; you were watching what?"

"I was watching Daddy fuck you."

"And what else were you doing?"

She pulled gently but firmly on my hair, forcing me to look up into her face. "And what else were you doing?" she asked again, her eyes nearly glowing with lust.

"I was touching myself," I said.

"Don't tell me, tell Daddy."

Daddy had gotten off the bed and come around in front of me. He was slowly jerking himself off in my face. I looked up at him, now, too. God, he looked hot. I confessed to him in my tiniest voice, "I was touching myself while I watched you fuck her."

Daddy seemed to be in a swoon. He stuck the head of his cock between my lips. Arching my head back uncomfortably with one hand, he worked his thick tool in and out of my mouth.

Louise worked two fingers up my hole then, giving me a thorough finger-fucking while Daddy worked on my eager mouth. Within moments, Daddy had pulled a condom from his pocket.

"It's Daddy's turn to punish you now," he explained. "I want you to kneel on the edge of the bed and lick Louise's pussy." He slathered some gooey lube on his sheathed dick. "You're to lick her until she comes, you understand me? No fingers, just lick her. Lick her while Daddy punishes you."

I understood. Louise was laying flat across the bed now and I knelt between her spread legs. I began licking her swollen pussy with gusto, centering on her tiny, erect clit.

But Daddy's idea of punishment was sublime. As I knelt between Louise's legs, my smarting red ass at the edge of the bed, my panties around my knees and my schoolgirl uniform shoved up around my waist, Daddy reamed my ass. He went at my hole aggressively, going in deep and pulling out slow, thoroughly opening the hole, giving me the fucking of my life.

It was my turn to moan into Louise's snatch while she writhed around on my tongue. She kept my face pressed close to her mound while my tongue licked furiously at her clit, wiggled it and swirled it. It didn't take much, really, to make her come. Daddy was grunting, seriously riding my ass in the depths of his own orgasm when Louise came in my mouth. I came just moments after she did, feeling positively delirious.

But the downside of it all was that shortly after this little explosion of mutual climaxes, they paid me my fee and told me I was free to go, even though it was obvious that they were in no hurry to leave. That's when Mr. Santos's idea of what our relationship consisted of became brutally clear to me. I was still just a hooker to him, just one that he had an unusual amount of fun with.

It had been a rude awakening for me, one that made me less inclined to arrange many trysts with him afterward. I never let on to him that Mrs. Hamilton had once been my high school teacher, or that it had been an unnerving liaison for me in a number of ways. I kept my thoughts to myself and went through the motions of earning my five hundred bucks. Eventually, I stopped seeing him altogether.

But yesterday, watching his casket disappear into the back of the hearse as I stood in the chill of the drizzling rain, I wished I'd spent just a little more time fucking him. I was going to miss that guy. I felt lucky I'd known him at all.

Endings

JULIA MOORE

With one hand placed firmly on the delicate swanlike curve of my neck, Josh pinned me down to his mattress. My heart raced in the connection where skin met skin, and I knew that if he pressed any harder against my throat, I would not be able to breathe. Did it make me scared? Did it make me scream?

No, baby, it made me come.

"You like that?" he whispered, hot breath on me, gold-brown eyes focused intently on my face. I couldn't have answered if I tried, my voice silenced by the placement of his steady palm. But my body trembled as a rush of pleasure slid through me. Without words, I told him everything he needed to know—told him more than I should have. The sweet scent of my arousal surrounded us, and I sighed and bucked my hips forward, wanting him inside me.

"You like being bad."

This was a statement, not a question, because we both knew he spoke the truth. Want proof?

In the room right next door, my angelic blond boyfriend slept peacefully alone in his bed. Beneath the translucent skin of his shut lids, he watched the G-rated movies of his dreams. As Josh fucked me, I visualized Daniel sleeping. During our six months together, I had memorized his rhythms; the way he started the evening restlessly, tossing one strong arm over my slim body and spooning in order to feel my heat. After several minutes, his breathing would grow deeper as his subconscious drew him in. Then he'd be practically unwakeable. Police helicopters cruising the Hollywood Hills around us would not make him stir. Sirens howling from the Sunset Strip could not rouse him. There was no way he'd even notice that I'd slipped from his embrace and from his bed, padded naked and barefoot down the brown shag seventies-style rug to Josh's room, and—

Josh told me how it worked. When Daniel and I made love, he would stand on the other side of the wall listening for the silent sound of gossamer fabric moving slowly along lean bare thighs. Josh would picture Daniel sliding my panties down and tossing them aside. Holding his breath, he would strain to make out the inaudible noises of lips meeting.

With one strong hand on his hard, throbbing cock, Josh would tug fiercely. His deep brown eyes would close, his head would fall forward, his handsome face contorting into an expression of such intensity that it resembled pain. Alone and stealthy, he would finally come in a rush into a different pair of silky panties, but ones that belonged to me, nonetheless.

Thrusting hard, his breath catching in his throat, and—

And—

Daniel was the cuckold in this dramedy, not knowing that when he kissed my heat-flushed skin it had already been kissed by Josh mere hours before. Never guessing that when he put his cock up there inside me, where it was warm and wet and ready, his tool was dampened not only by the sticky juices of my come but by the evidence of his roommate's spent pleasure.

"I love you, Tasha," Daniel would sigh into my shiny black hair. "I love you, honey, and—"

And—

And this is not the start of the story.

Josh was bad news. The type of bad news most women can see coming from a distance. You'd have thought I would know better. No neophyte in the world of dating, at twenty-six I'd been making the romantic rounds for enough years to spot a soap opera in the making and to figure out how to avoid being the star. But I missed the signs. Can't say why. I would have liked to believe that I'd be immune to men like Josh. I worked in Hollywood. Insert the cynical laugh track here.

Maybe it was Josh's appearance. Just my type, he stood a sinewy six foot two, with dark curly hair, mesmerizing eyes, and sharp, foxy features. You got the feeling, watching him move, that he was well-hung. In downtown bars, as he made his way through the crowded room to the jukebox, both men and women turned to watch him. Yet with all that subtle power, Josh remained someone you might have considered hooking up with on an island getaway, but nothing permanent. He was not the type of person from whom you'd want to accept a check.

And still, I fell.

"You're like me," Josh said flatly one afternoon when we were by ourselves, "just like me."

"I'm not."

"You're too close. You can't see it." Sitting at my side on the lipstick-red leather sofa, Josh brought his hand to my thigh, and his fingers began running up and down the length of my leg from the lace-edged hem of my dress to my knee. "You use people up for your own pleasure."

"I don't," I told him, not sure who I believed, not liking the way he was staring at me, as if seeing me for the first time.

He slid his hand under my dress. "You're using him. You don't love him."

Daniel liked to kiss the nape of my neck and say my scent intoxicated him. When we were apart, he kept a pair of my cherry-printed panties in his pocket and he'd finger them at inappropriate times. During an important meeting with clients. When talking with a neighbor. In line at the grocery store. It excited him, something semi-naughty to give him a bad boy thrill. He wasn't a bad boy. He was sweet and good and kind and Josh hated him for all of those reasons.

"You think about me when you fuck him," Josh said.

"We don't fuck." The word was wrong for describing what Daniel and I did, and it sounded harsh coming from my lips.

"Make love, then. Whatever."

"Whatever," I repeated, wondering why I didn't push his hand aside.

"You're bad," he said next, continuing the trip with his

probing fingers, speaking in a soft croon that I recognized from hearing him talk to women on the phone. It was his come-on voice, "Come on, sweetheart, let me see you tonight…." His come-fuck-me voice, "Why don't you come on over here. We can just watch movies. We don't have to do anything…."

"I'm not bad," I said, immediately recognizing the statement as a lie. *This* was bad, wasn't it? My panties were drenched, and I leaned back on the crimson leather couch as Josh's relentless fingers found the source of my pleasure. In my head, I heard my voice continue: I am not a good person, despite the fact that everyone always said that I was. Maybe I believed their hype for a while. Maybe I thought that if someone said it enough times it would come true. But Josh's hands found out my secret. Daniel was kind, but Josh was my mirror image.

Sliding off the sofa, Josh got between my legs. Slowly, he reached both hands under my pale blue summer dress and took hold of the waistband of my satin panties and with his eyes locked on mine, he started to pull them down. It was up to me now. Would I lift my ass and help him? Or would I squirm away, call him a bastard, and flee back to the safety of an honest, loving relationship?

In a single move, I sealed my fate.

As I raised my hips, Josh gave me a look that let me know he'd won. Moving quickly now, he pulled my panties down and tucked them into his pocket.

"Daniel has one pair and I'll have another. When you are next to him in bed, think of that. When you're fucking…" and then he gave me an evil half-grin, "I mean, when you're doing whatever it is you two do, think of me rubbing these panties on my cock and coming."

And then he spread my thighs with his warm fingertips and leaned forward, pressing his mouth firmly against my pussy. Head back against the sofa, I groaned, letting loose that deep animalistic sound of pure pleasure. Some men know. They just *know*. His tongue made lazy spirals, then deep circles. His fingertips slipped in my juices as he spread my nether lips wide apart. Up and down his tongue traced, teasing me. The harsh scratch of his evening shadow touched my inner thighs, and this sent me over the edge. No soft peach fuzz like Daniel's. The caress of his tongue combined with the roughness of his whiskers made me come.

That was the beginning, the afternoon when my world went topsy-turvy as I embarked on that well-traveled route of the cheat. I lied. I manipulated. I did the dangerous dance that is the beginning of every broken heart. When Daniel left for work at his upstanding job as an entertainment lawyer, Josh would come into the bed with me. Would take me the way I craved. Working me hard. Teasing until I could barely breathe. We would look at each other and I could see in his eyes what his plans were, would know a beat before it happened what he was going to do next.

Cool metal handcuffs held my wrists in place. A leather belt found its snakelike way up and down my thighs. Never leaving marks. Never truly hurting me. Just putting the possibilities out there, like a menu of erotic assortments from which I could someday choose. "I could give you what you want," Josh promised. "All you have to do is say the word."

I'd never felt a connection like that. Never felt a jealousy like I did when he brought one of his other sluts home to fuck.

Daniel and I would sit on that same battered red sofa, watching a made-for-TV movie, raising the volume so that we wouldn't have to hear the moans from Josh's room.

My boyfriend's blond eyebrows would lift as he'd look over at me. As if to say, "Can you believe it? Can you believe someone would actually make noises like that?"

And I'd think to myself how I had made those same sexy, sultry sounds only hours before. Spread out like melting butter on Josh's mattress. My limbs weak. My breath coming in short, staccato bursts.

Hours later, at a more appropriate bedtime, Daniel and I would take our turns in the bathroom. Washing up. Brushing our teeth. Then we would retreat to his room with our minty-fresh breath and our clean bodies, and on his king-sized mattress we would make the soft, sweet love we were accustomed to. His hands roaming over my face, fingers pressed against my bottom lip so that I could flick out my tongue and kiss the tips as he entered me. There were never any sudden moves. Never any unexpected tricks.

My mind would be focused on the goings-on in the room next door. Was Josh awake? Was he listening? Was he laughing at me?

What I couldn't figure out was how long we could keep up the farce. If I broke up with Daniel, I'd still want to see Josh. Would it work between us without the danger? Without the risk of being caught? I didn't know, and I wasn't willing to find out. Selfishly, I used Daniel as an unknowing partner in this three-way charade. At least, that's what I thought.

But who was using who?

One evening, Josh was dateless. Amazingly, he joined our duo on the sofa. He sat on one side, Daniel on the other. We were a sin sandwich, with me so consumed with my filthy thoughts that I no longer had any idea what movie we were watching. Both men were casually pressed against me, leg to leg, thigh to thigh. I knew that Josh was aware of my skin, of my heat, pressing into him. But was Daniel?

When I caught the reflection of our threesome in a framed painting across the way, I tried to decipher the message there. Decadent or deranged? I couldn't be sure. All I knew was that my pussy tightened each time one of my men shifted positions. That I would shift myself in order to regain contact between both of them. All I wanted was what I couldn't have. Finally, Daniel interlocked his fingers with mine, said goodnight to Josh, and led me from the room.

It was earlier than usual, and I was surprised when he herded me directly into his bedroom without the standard routine of getting washed and ready. With no explanation, he lifted me in his arms and set me down in the center of his bed. Slowly, carefully, he undid the ties at the top of my dress, pulled the slim sheath off my body and tossed it to the floor. Just as carefully, he undid my strapless bra, pulled off my sheer nylon panties. And then for a moment, he simply stared.

Guilt flooded through me. Was he looking for evidence that I'd been bad, staring at a road map of my deceit? Did he know the places that Josh most liked to kiss? The backs of my knees. The slight indents at the tops of my thighs. Were there any pale lilac bruises left from where Josh held me too tight?

Without a word, Daniel stripped out of his clothes, tossing his white T-shirt onto the floor, kicking off his faded jeans. Then he pushed me onto my side, sliding me so that I was dead in the center of the mattress. His eyes locked with mine, he drove into me, a hard thrust, hands gripping my shoulders, grunting with the effort as he fucked me. *Fucked.* That word was in my head. Something so different from being sweetly taken, being partners in an action. No, Daniel was fucking me, and I couldn't believe how wet the thought made me...or how much wetter I grew when a second set of hands took hold of me from behind. What was going on?

"Shh, Tasha," Josh whispered. "Don't even think...."

I couldn't. There I was, in between my two men, my body shaking fiercely as Josh licked in a line down my spine to the curve of my asscheeks. *Don't think*, my mind repeated. *Don't even think.* His hands gently opened me up and I felt his hot breath warming my asshole before his tongue slid deep inside me. This was something that he liked to do, an act I'd always thought that Daniel would never have even considered. Wetness flooded through me. The feeling of being taken from one side, and filled in the other was almost too much. I moaned, a harsh, almost barking sound that I didn't even recognize as my own voice.

"That's right," Josh said, moving away just long enough to guide me along. "That's the way," and then I realized it wasn't him talking. It was Daniel. And another thought exploded through my mind. Daniel had heard us. Daniel had stood on the other side of the wall and listened as Josh pressed me up against the cold plaster and fucked me. Who was playing who? Who was the real cuckold? I had no idea. No reason to care. All I had was a reason to come.

But before I could, Daniel moved us, sliding out of me

and taking over from where Josh had begun, strong hands stretching me open, mouth hungry. Why had I thought he'd be shocked by this action? His lips parted, his tongue ran in a line from my pussy to my rear hole, and then he was sucking me, probing me, while I just closed my eyes and sighed. Josh had moved to let Daniel in, and now he took the opportunity of my open mouth to slip his rock-hard cock inside. I was sucked and sucking, not thinking anymore, not caring, just letting myself be moved again, as Daniel rotated my body so that he was on the bottom and I was on the top. Astride him. Riding.

As if we were part of a well-choreographed dance team, Josh moved away as Daniel thrust into my slippery-wet pussy. I could feel him on the bed with me, but I didn't know where he was going. I just stared at my boyfriend as he reached up and stroked his fingertips along the front of my body. His hands found out my nipples, pinched them tightly, and I groaned. Fingers tightening around my nipples, Daniel gave me the dark spark of pain that I always crave. Pleasure spiked with pain makes me come like nothing else. But how did he know? Had Josh told him what I liked, clued him in to all the different sensations that take me to that higher level? Or was it obvious now, with all the shells broken and crumbling around us so that only the inner core remained. Could anyone have looked at me and known exactly what I liked?

Don't even think, I told myself as I pumped my body up and down his throbbing cock, working him as Josh, now in back of me again, licked from the base of my spine down lower...lower...so that I could feel his warm breath but not his tongue. Where was he going? What was he doing? It didn't take me long to figure that out.

He was lapping at Daniel's balls. I understood this from the expression in my boyfriend's gray-green eyes. That joyous expression of doing something…oh, not wrong. Because who decides what's right and wrong? Not dirty. But ultimate. The ultimate pleasure. Watching Daniel's eyelashes flutter, his full lips part, his body arch, I felt myself reaching that place with him. And as Daniel said his lover's name in a rush of breath as he came, my heart started to pound.

"Oh, fuck—" he said. "Oh, sweetheart," he said, "Oh, *Josh*," he said, and—

And—

And this is not the end of the story.

Third Party
DAWN M. PARES

Maybe twice a year she'll rent a car and pick him up in the
parking lot outside the plant. She always drives, even if Len
picks the place. He's been picking up extra shifts, and he'd
stayed late waiting for Frank to come back from the emergency
room where they'd sewn Jorge's pinky back on.

He hears gravel crunch under the wheels as she pulls up
next to him in a midsized sedan, looking like a cool breeze in
a short (but not *too* short) ice-blue satin dress with spaghetti
straps. He grins at her and she pretends to ignore him. Like
she's a bus driver and he's just another fare.

It's after eight already, and he's beat. It'll be at least two
hours before they get anywhere. He pushes the seat back as
far as it'll go and settles back to breathe in the new car smell.
It smells bland and anonymous, the way hotel rooms should
smell but never do. It smells like it's been put together by

robots, and for some reason that makes him think of his dad, with his blue work shirt rolled up over his arms and grease under his nails.

He naps a little, lets Susan wind them down the freeway to the bigger suburbs. He knows she's packed a bag for him, and that he'll shower and maybe shave, maybe not, when they get to the hotel. The chances are good she'll have bought some new lingerie, and that maybe she's rolled it up in his boxers so that even their underwear gets a little action on this trip. He smiles to himself, eyes closed in the car, the hum of the road beneath them and Susan tapping her fresh manicure against the wheel at lights and tolls. She never plays the radio on the way there.

Later, in the car again, Len wears a clean T-shirt under his jacket, his hair spiked high. When he'd held up his razor, Susan had studied him a moment before shaking her head. He's looking for a place on Dean that he'd overheard the new secretary talking about. Mitzi'd spent most of her lunch hour bitching to Gina about her boyfriend and all the dives he'd dragged her to in the great state of Minnesota.

He finally sees it, and decides it looks about right. He taps the window and glances at Susan, who lifts her chin, trying to find a parking space.

He'd counted on Mitzi to exaggerate and, once he and Susan have parked the car and wandered inside, he sees that the place isn't half bad. A crowd of regulars at the bar, some empty booths, low light and enough smoke to feel like ambience. Susan still looks too good for the scarred wooden stools, but

Len fits right in. He catches a few eyes right out of the gate, but then he and Susan always turn heads.

It's early, and the crowds won't be along for another hour or so. He knocks on the counter and orders a Dos Equis and a Honey Brown, then leaves her at the bar so he can take a leak.

By the time he's washed up and on his way back, some smooth talker's already doing the lean on Susan.

Len strolls up behind her and rests a hand on her shoulder. He can feel her smile, and he smiles too, the one that's all attitude and teeth. He tips his head a little, and waits to see what the guy's gonna do about it. Susan laces a hand around his back underneath his jacket and plucks at his T-shirt.

Smooth Talker goes a little pale and backs off. He remembers to take his beer with him. Susan nestles close for a moment, tucking three fingers in the waist of Len's jeans. Then she sits up straight again, and takes her arm back. Len kisses her hair and eases away. He decides to take a circuit around the room, see what he can see. He remembers to take his beer with him, too.

The kid's pretty, all big eyes and long legs. He's twenty-one or twenty-two maybe, but he's not new at this, and when he bumps shoulders with Len at the bar, Len counts to three before he sees the guy smile.

"Davie."

"Len."

"You from out of town?"

Len smiles back after his own pause, toying with his empty beer bottle.

"Just driving through, yeah. Staying the night."

Davie shifts closer, and Len can feel his hip and thigh scrape his jeans. The guy leans forward, hands spread on the bar, and smiles sideways, showing teeth just as pretty as the rest of him. When his eyes hit the light right, they're the same color as the beer in his mug.

"Wanna play some pool?"

"Nah. Wanna make out?"

The kid laughs into his drink.

"Yeah. Okay."

The kid's hair is brown, and long enough to touch the collar of his plain white T-shirt. Len sets his beer bottle down and makes for the restrooms in the back; the overhead lamp in the short hallway that leads to the john is out and it's as good a place as any to see what the kid has under his hood. He leans back against the wall that's lumpy with scraped paint and old band stickers and waits for Davie to finish his beer.

When he shows up, tall as hell and walking cowboy slow in his low-slung jeans, Len lowers his head and checks him out under his lashes. Davie lounges against the wall beside him and sticks his hands in his pockets.

"You could blow me in the stalls," Davie says.

Len grins in the half-dark. He likes this kid.

"Don't wanna."

"You got a hotel room?"

"What's your hurry?" He gives a half turn, shoulder wedged against the wall, one hand against the wall so his arm closes Davie in. "You could be a shitty kisser."

The guy knows a challenge when he hears one, and that big, soft mouth sips a breath out of him before pushing a slick, beer-bitter tongue past his teeth.

Len finds himself pushing at him, trying to tug him closer and half-climb him. For his part, Davie kisses like he's drowning and Len has all the air. It's fun, if you don't miss breathing.

He has no idea how long they've been at it before Susan finds them.

She doesn't even clear her throat. The tap of her expensive shoes on the beer-warped floorboards is enough.

Davie jumps like he's been goosed. Len snorts and grins at Susan.

She arches one eyebrow and tips her head. Len shrugs a little, then slings a companionable arm around the kid's shoulders. She gives the guy an assessing stare like the one she used before nixing Len's shave, and then steps in real close. She has to lean her head back, because the kid's taller than Len is, but she seems to like what she sees.

Len can feel that old sweet tingle come back. It makes him restless. He watches Susan rest the flat of one hand against Davie's chest, then slide her hand up and cup the back of his neck. Davie looks mildly freaked, but he doesn't bolt. He looks over at Len, who nods once, and back at Susan, all glints of gold in the shitty light in the alcove by the men's room. He looks down at Susan, who's skating another hand up his chest, and Len can see him decide before he lowers his head to kiss her. She doesn't let him, but she presses her fingers against his soft mouth and says, "You can come."

Len doesn't like first-timers much. It's a lot of work, a lot of hand-holding, and he has to give them rules. He hates that shit.

But Davie's not new to sex, only to the third party cha-cha, and Len figures he'll be a quick study.

"You don't touch her."

And really, that's the only rule that counts. So far as Len knows, no one's touched Susan but him in ten years of marriage, two of those years including picking up strays in suburban bars.

Davie nods, his long brown hair falling in his face. His mouth has been slightly open since they got to the room, and he keeps glancing back to Len, his pink tongue making that soft mouth gleam.

Len takes his chin in his hand and pulls Davie down for a kiss, licking the guy's lips for him.

"Good boy. Second rule: you do as she says. That's not negotiable."

He tugs Davie's shirt up and off and pats the top of his head.

Davie's all tan and smooth and Len can count his ribs, but he's still got twenty, thirty pounds on Len. His big brown eyes are soft and a little wild. "Now listen up, we're not going to hurt you. We don't play rough. But you have to play by our rules."

Davie nods, and reaches out for Len's belt.

Len shoves his hand away. "Wait. Wait for Susan, kid."

Davie's got a long, pretty, narrow face and shoulders as wide as two Lens. He's got a little stubble on his pointed chin, but that just makes his mouth look softer. He grins a little and leans back on the bed, feet set.

"I don't usually do two at a time."

"And you won't be, buddy. We're here for Susan. She's the brains, here. I'm just pretty." He grins back at the kid and Davie shakes his hair out of his eyes.

"You can start, Len."

Susan's in the ugly-ass armchair, her legs crossed at the ankle, as polite and composed as a talk-show host.

Len never looks away from Davie and shucks his jacket and then his T-shirt. He stands between Davie's spread knees and the kid waits.

"You can touch him now, Davie. Until I tell you to stop."

Davie sits up and folds his fingers in the pockets of Len's jeans, dragging him close.

Len likes his lean face, the way he smells like beer.

"You wanna suck me?" Len asks.

Davie shakes his head.

"You looking to get fucked, Davie?"

Davie fishes out an accordion of condoms from his own pocket and starts unbuttoning his jeans.

Len's never been one to enjoy a chatty Cathy, and he decides he likes Davie. Len's barefoot and unzipped before the other guy's even rolled over. Susan stands now, and hands him a little bottle of KY.

Davie, bare-assed, kneels on the coverlet, face already rubbing into the pillow. His back expands and drops with long slow breaths, and Len figures this is some kind of Zen sex trick when he tests the guy with a finger.

Nice.

Not a lot of prep here, and that's just fine.

He sees the kid start when Susan's cool hand strokes his back. She's cocking her head as if deciding to rearrange him.

"Look at me, Davie." Her voice is so low and soft Len almost doesn't recognize it.

Len bets she likes the way Davie's hair keeps falling in his face. His mouth is so fucking red, and his face looks sharp enough to cut her hand when she cups his cheek.

"Is there anything you want?"

Davie just blinks at her. Len can see the guy's breath making his hair flutter a little by his mouth.

"She means, anything specific? You want it hard? You want me to kiss you some more? You want to call me Daddy?" He waggles his eyebrows, and the kid shakes his head, smothers a laugh in the pillow.

Then he's craning his neck over one shoulder, eyes glinting. "I want it hard. But I'll call you Daddy if you really want me to, mister."

Len grins, the kind of grin that makes people back away, but Davie has to know he's only having a good time. Fun times. The *best*.

He kneels on the bed behind the kid and Davie drops his head, bracing his arms.

"Start slow, Len." Susan's voice is cool and steady, and he nods absently. Davie's arms relax, and that's when Len pushes in.

"Fffffuck—" Davie's already breathless, and Len's a little crazy: alive with the kid's heat, with the sinking mattress beneath his knees, the cool mechanical breeze of the hotel swirling around his shoulders, and the soft drift of Susan, her perfume weaving around him like smoke as she paces beside them.

Davie's legs are long and skinny, but hard against his own thighs. He rears back a little, resting his hands on Davie's hips, not hanging on yet.

He's working his way into a rhythm; he closes his eyes and lifts his chin. Rock and roll. The old fuck. It's all his, and everything that's his is Susan's and this is for both of them. The kid might as well not even be there. Except...he is.

Len opens his eyes to see Davie's sweat-slicked back, the flush making the skin a pretty color you never see anywhere else.

Even moving slow, Len can feel the action build. Can feel his heart rate climb right up. He rocks again, deep, trying to be slow, and there's Susan's hand against his throat.

"Lean forward and kiss him...here."

She trails her fingertip along the ridge of the guy's spine and Len obeys.

Davie is crooning softly, taking shaky little breaths, and he's muttering into his pillow and Susan's petting Len's hair, and then the little tug that means, "Look at me, Len."

So he does. She's his whole world, all cool blue, like a girl-shaped ocean with the sun in her hair.

Len's dripping sweat and her nails are hard against his skin, at his shoulder, in his hair, and he strains for her, and the boy gasps.

She kisses him, and he closes his eyes so he can taste her better, and he's working Davie hard now, he's pounding him and somehow Susan hangs on to him, in no hurry.

The kid's getting louder, and Len hides his face against the soft skin of Susan's throat for just a moment before she lets him go.

"Make him come, Len."

The bed isn't so big that he can't feel her when she lies down beside them.

Her hair is smooth, her hands are relaxed, and she's watching Davie's dick bounce as the kid pants under him.

She reaches out and strokes Davie's belly, and Len wants to lick the sweat from her palm. Urgent little moans from Davie now and Len can hear him cursing actual words.

Susan rolls on her side to watch them both, her brows furrowed as she studies them. Her other hand wipes along the kid's back, now, and Len feels Davie's body stutter, throw the rhythm and catch it again.

Len presses her hand against the other man's back and his knuckles are white on Davie's hip.

"Come on, motherfucker, she wants you to *come*—" His own voice is collapsing, and his jaw is locked. Fuck fuck fuck fuck is the only thing his body knows; words are for later, and before.

Finally, he can feel the little jolt that means Davie is coming.

Susan lifts her hand from the blanket beneath Davie's heaving body, showing Len he's done his job: her free hand is striped with white.

Len is nodding, and trying to stop.

He can feel Davie sighing, and slacking down.

"Fun," Len murmurs, pulling out. He knots the empty condom out of habit and crawls past the kid's gangly body toward Susan.

"You can watch. And you can touch me," Susan says. Davie, flushed, his hair tacked to his face with sweat, gives her a lazy, bashful grin. Len doesn't think about what she's said until Susan turns her head and meets Len's eyes as he kneels over her.

There's something cautious and cool in her eyes, and it's a challenge, and it's an order, and it's just the two of them in the room again, inhale-exhale and the decision has been made. And made without him.

Len doesn't nod, tries not to let on that he's bugged, just reaches out and takes Davie's big, knuckly hand and slides it down along Susan's belly and the fabric of her silky dress, and then guides that hand underneath her rucked-up skirt.

Her mouth is glossy and pink, like candy that's already been sucked on.

He can see her shiver, see her hair fan out on the pillow, see her throat flash, making the tiny links of her gold necklace shift.

She arches a little when Davie curls his fingers against her, and Len knows just how wet she is, remembers it from a thousand times alone with her, knows the wet, soft throb of her, that feeling like you could sink right through her to the other side....

She's breathing harder now, her eyes all silvery, locked with his.

There's no one else for Susan.

Len's the only one in the room, she proves it with every little gasp, even though Len's not touching her at all.

He bends his elbows so he can hover over her, touches the nipple of her left breast, peaked under her thin dress, with his breath. Then his lips. Then his teeth.

Her cheeks are pink now, streaks of color along her neck — she gets blotchy when she's hot, and fuck, it turns him on—

He can feel Davie's arm brush against his dick as Davie works his wife.

The wiry hairs there only remind him of Susan, and he can have her now, she's ready for him.

"Say it, Susan. Say it."

Her eyes are glazed and wild but she never looks away.

He parts her lips with his thumb, feels the slick edge of her teeth.

"You've gotta say it, Suze," he reminds her.

She bites his thumb, hard, and he yanks it away, laughing.

He strokes one hand up along her thigh, pushing her dress up higher, and she finally closes her eyes, shaking her head.

"Susan."

She bucks a little, and Davie's hand never slows down or speeds up.

Finally, she can't take it anymore.

"Please—"

Her eyebrows are tense, her face is peach-pink and warm against his own cheek and he sighs her name in her ear, soothes her, promises her, and finally, finally fucks her—

Len almost hates it, it's so strong. The deep-sigh relief of it, because he always worries she'll change her mind.

Her thighs wrap around his and she brings her hands up to push against the headboard.

She makes desperate little sobs, and she pushes so fiercely against him that there have been times she's shoved him right off the bed.

Len never notices when Davie takes his hand back, he only knows when Susan comes like a clenched fist around him, and that's when he's allowed to let go.

"Love you love you—"

She never hears him.

She tosses her head, as if she thinks he's a liar, and she always *always* looks angry when they're done.

But it's only for a second.

Len pets her hair, touches her lower lip with his thumb when she's quiet.

She opens her eyes again and her whole face is shining. Susan glows in the dark.

But the hotel room has two old yellow lamps, and Len remembers the kid beside them and he and Susan both turn their heads toward him at the same time.

"You can go now," Susan tells him.

Len stands up when Davie does, and they tug their jeans on in tandem.

Len zips up and holds out a hand to Davie before he pulls his shirt back over his head. Davie gives him a wary look before smiling slightly and shaking Len's hand.

"Had fun." Davie holds still and then finally nods.

"Me too," he says.

Len locks the door behind him, and when he turns around, Susan is already in the shower.

In the morning, she'll wake him up wearing the new lingerie for the twenty seconds it'll take him to unhitch it, and they'll fuck until they rinse off in the twenty minutes before checkout.

Len usually drives them back.

Susan's in loose cotton slacks and a snug gray T-shirt. One of Len's. She ignores him on the drive home, thumbing through some briefs she packed along with her undies.

She lets him choose the music. It used to bug her that he was always restlessly searching the dial, but now she never seems to hear even the *good* songs.

Soon, they'll hit town and have breakfast for lunch (never fucking *brunch*) at Patsio's, a little Greek diner they've been going to since they used to soak away hangovers with French toast and root beer floats, first at four in the morning, and then again after they'd crawled out of bed. One black-and-white (split in half) and a box full of (always stale) baklava for later.

She'll order eggs and make notes for court in the morning, and he'll eat her home fries and his own plate of French toast, and remember when she used to lick the powdered sugar off his fingertips right there in the booth.

The New Fiancée

N. T. MORLEY

Meredith got home from work around midnight and discovered the beautiful woman sitting in the living room. It took her a moment to register her surprise, especially given the casual comfort with which the woman sat on the couch sipping a glass of red wine. The woman, a strikingly tall and quite breathtaking ivory-skinned brunette, was very dressed up—much like Meredith herself—as if she were about to spend the night at the opera, or had just finished doing so. The woman's dress, long and black, was slit on both sides almost up to her hips, revealing the full length of her shapely legs. The dress was also low-cut and showed that the woman had quite ample, perfect endowments. Perhaps in her midthirties, she was strikingly beautiful, her jet-black hair and pale skin accenting her rather Nordic features.

"Hello," Meredith said nervously.

"You must be Meredith," said the woman, without getting up. She looked Meredith over quite blatantly, not even trying to disguise the up-and-down motion of her eyes that focused first on Meredith's face, then slid down her body, then slowly stroked upward to rest on the single slit in Meredith's dress—not quite as high as that in the strange woman's dress, but more than revealing enough to show what shapely legs the girl had—then continued up to take in the slight swell of Meredith's small but perfect bust. Meredith felt her face getting hot as the woman's eyes lingered over her breasts, then slowly rose to meet Meredith's gaze, fixing her with a hungry stare.

"I've heard a lot about you," said the woman.

"Ah, Meredith," said Phillip, appearing from the kitchen with a Scotch in one hand and a bottle of wine in the other. "We've been waiting for you." He topped off the woman's drink and sat down opposite her on the big white armchair, propping his feet on the coffee table quite indelicately and taking a sip of his Scotch.

"You remember me telling you about Yvanna, my ex-wife?"

Meredith gave a shiver.

"Please, Phillip, *former* wife. Ex-wife sounds so unfriendly."

"We're anything but that, my dear," said Phillip with a lustful glance at Yvanna. He then looked at Meredith with the kind of lascivious sense of ownership he always gave her when he knew he would soon prove just how profoundly he had his new fiancée under his control.

"With our wedding date set, I figured it was time for you and Yvanna to get…acquainted."

Again, Meredith shivered. She saw Yvanna's eyes flickering over her once more with the immodest gaze of the heartless seducer suddenly set loose upon an ingénue, and knew immediately what was to be expected of her.

As if to assert her independence, Meredith quickly assessed Yvanna's body, attempting to display the same kind of unrepentant randiness that the self-composed woman showed toward her. She could see the older woman's sensuous curves, the firmness of her full breasts capped by hard nipples tenting the thin fabric of the black opera dress. Meredith let her eyes caress those perfect tits, knowing that within moments she would be called upon to touch them, kiss them, perhaps even suckle them, before being bidden to travel further into depravity and perform services foreign to her. She knew she would be expected to touch the woman lower down, between the slits of that dress and, without a doubt, underneath the dress itself. That, she could not even comprehend; her head spun at the very thought of it. It was all Meredith could do to look at the woman's breasts and know she would soon be touching them. But those bright green eyes of hers did not linger on Yvanna's ample tits; on the contrary, Meredith let her eyes drift upward to Yvanna's piercing, frosty blue gaze and, unable to keep up her façade of self-confidence, whimpered softly and dropped her eyes submissively.

She could feel her nipples hardening under her dress, standing out plainly through the thin satin, as if advertising to the woman the effect she was having on her.

"That's a very nice dress," said Yvanna with a smile, her eyes lingering on Meredith's chest. "I hear you're a hostess at a chi-chi restaurant. I'm surprised they let you wear a dress like that. Much less without a bra."

Meredith wanted very badly to cross her arms in front of her. Her arms even twitched involuntarily, as if seeking a chance to cover her embarrassment. But Meredith did not let herself hide her breasts from Yvanna's devouring gaze. Phillip had long since forbidden her that privilege. Instead, she stood there, her nipples hardening even more under Yvanna's stare, a quiver starting deep in her body as she nervously answered.

"Th—thank you, Ma'am. The...the owner says it helps bring the customers in."

"The owner? Is he the one who told you it was all right to wear that dress without a bra?"

Meredith's face grew hotter as she blushed uncontrollably.

"Yes, Ma'am, but that's not why I wear it that way," said Meredith. "My Master told me to wear it this way."

"Phillip, you dog. You're just like you always were. If anything, you're worse. Remember when you sent me to court wearing that see-through dress?"

"I remember," said Phillip.

"And no bra or panties at all," Yvanna sighed. "I thought the judge was going to charge me with contempt. Luckily, he was a man of liberal tastes. Just a few moments alone in his chambers and I was back in the court's favors."

"You never told me that," Phillip snapped.

"Mmmm, didn't I?" smiled Yvanna. "Yes, it was a striking example of judicial corruption, and quite a lot of fun. Lucky for me it's too late for you to punish me." Turning back to Meredith, Yvanna smiled and said, "Phillip used to send me all sorts of places without panties." She paused and smiled broadly at Meredith. "You *are* wearing panties, aren't you, dear?"

"Y-yes, Ma'am," said Meredith. "Just—just a thong."

"A thong. Let me see, dear."

Meredith's eyes went to her Master, whether to check if it was all right or to beg not to do it, Phillip didn't notice or care.

"My ex-wife and I are very close, darling. Show her your panties."

Meredith began to lift her dress, nervously feeling the satin bunch in her grasp. She brought the dress up to her waist, revealing her miniscule white lace thong, which barely covered her pussy and showed quite clearly that it was shaved smooth. The crotch of the garment was so small that Meredith's full pussy lips, now unaccountably swollen, squeezed around the sides, revealing the piercings Phillip had placed there.

"Come here, darling. Let me have a closer look."

Meredith nervously walked to Yvanna's side, and with a glance at Phillip, knew what was expected.

Meredith lifted her foot and placed her high-heeled shoe on the coffee table, leaving her legs spread.

"My, my," Yvanna said, reaching out to stroke the moist crotch of the thong. Meredith stifled a whimper as Yvanna touched her. "Such pretty things you buy your slaves nowadays, Phillip. And such pretty jewelry." Yvanna's long, slender fingers slid under the crotch of the thong and teased Meredith's pierced lips apart. Meredith gasped and let out a long, low moan as Yvanna slid two fingers into her. She struggled to remain standing, knowing that to fail to do so would bring punishment. Perhaps a spanking, or worse.

Meredith could not bear the thought of being punished in front of her Master's ex-wife.

"She's soaking, darling. She's positively gushing. She's your own little blonde tsunami. Phillip, is she more of an exhibitionist than I was? Does showing her tits off all night turn your little slave on *this* much?"

"I don't know," chuckled Phillip. "Ask her."

Yvanna's eyes locked with Meredith's, and the older woman's two fingers slid deeper in, her thumb teasing the swollen nub of Meredith's pierced clitoris. Meredith let out a faint whine and bit her red-painted lip as she tried to stay standing.

"Does it, Meredith? Does it turn you on to show the customers your tits?"

Yvanna's thumb pressed firmly on Meredith's ringed clit, and Meredith bit her lip so hard that for a moment she thought she might have drawn blood.

She took a deep breath and managed to speak.

"Yes, Ma'am. It does turn me on. But that's not why I'm wet."

"Then why are you wet, darling?"

Meredith had had the best intentions of confessing it, knowing that no show of coyness would get her out of the evening's expected services. But now, she found her throat closing with embarrassment. Her face turned deep red, suddenly so hot that she felt she might pass out.

Yvanna chuckled.

"I know why you're wet, dear," said Yvanna. "It's because you know I'm going to fuck you. And you've never been with a woman before."

Meredith whimpered as Yvanna's fingers slid in and out of her cunt. It was the first time she'd ever been touched like that by a woman—the first time a woman had touched her there at all.

"Y-yes, Ma'am," said Meredith breathlessly.

Yvanna's hand came out of Meredith's cunt, and the younger woman let go of her dress, feeling the satin snake its way down her legs as Yvanna reached up to touch her face. Taller than Meredith by six or eight inches, Yvanna found it easy to reach Meredith's mouth with her fingers—but Meredith, well trained, still leaned down to make it easier on her. Meredith obediently parted her lips and accepted Yvanna's slick fingers into her mouth, licking them clean. She had done it so many times—been *trained* to do it—that it was second nature to her. But the taste of her cunt had always come to her ripe and fresh via Phillip's body—his fingers, his tongue, even his cock.

Never on a woman's fingers. But Meredith licked, hungrily, the taste of her own pussy sending tingles of electricity down into her body.

Yvanna's fingers came out of Meredith's suckling mouth glistening with spittle.

"There's no point in being a flirt about it, then," said Yvanna, her voice suddenly filled with command. "Take off your dress."

Meredith began to turn toward Phillip, but stopped when Yvanna's harsh voice snapped, "Meredith!" Meredith turned back to Yvanna, shocked, and the brunette's cold eyes froze Meredith to the bone.

"You've been given to me," she said. "If Phillip wants to

stop me, he will. For now, you do exactly what I tell you to do. And don't look to him for advice."

"Y-yes, Ma'am," Meredith whimpered.

"Now take off your dress before I take it off for you," said Yvanna.

Meredith felt a little quiver go through her at the harsh sound in Yvanna's voice. She had heard that same harshness many times in the voice of her Master, and it never failed to make her desperate to please him.

Meredith took her foot off the coffee table and turned more fully to face Yvanna. Her hands quivered as she reached up to the left strap of her dress and gently eased it over her shoulder. So insubstantial was the dress that one side of it immediately fell away, revealing Meredith's bare left breast with its firm, pink nipple plainly erect from arousal. Hesitating only slightly, Meredith eased the other strap off her shoulder, and the dress went sliding down to her waist, revealing both small but perfect breasts, showing by their glowing pearlescence that her Master never allowed her to sunbathe.

Meredith wriggled her hips, pushing the dress down over them. It slid down her thighs and pooled around her high-heeled shoes. Obediently, she stepped out of the dress, now naked except for her shoes and the quite-soaked thong.

"Lovely tits," said Yvanna. "Quite a nice body in general. Do you have her work out?"

"Two hours a day," said Phillip. "Mostly on her legs and abdomen."

"Yes, I see that," said Yvanna, running her hands down Meredith's slender legs. "She must be able to fuck like a demon." Meredith obediently leaned into her, allowing Yvanna to get a good, firm hold of the back of her thighs, where hours of Phillip's prescribed workout had built the perfect muscles for pushing herself onto his cock—or anything he chose.

Yvanna reached up and grabbed Meredith's bare ass with a slap, squeezing her firm buttocks tightly. Meredith could feel the pressure against her cunt, and caught her breath.

"Are you, dear?" Yvanna asked. "Are you a rollicking good lay, a fucking racehorse when there's a cock around?"

"I-I try, Ma'am," said Meredith nervously.

Yvanna polished off her red wine and leaned over to set the empty glass on the coffee table behind Meredith. "He always does it to you from behind, right? Never face to face."

"Y-yes, Ma'am," said Meredith, blushing furiously anew as she looked into Yvanna's eyes. "Only from behind. He only takes me from behind. I—" she paused, her voice quavering. "I've actually never been taken the other way. Face to face, I mean."

"Never?" smiled Yvanna. "Never in your life?"

"Never," said Meredith, dropping her eyes.

"Show me," said Yvanna with a smile, spinning Meredith around and pulling hard on the girl so she stumbled backward onto the sofa, legs spread and straddling Yvanna's lap. "Show me how you fuck."

Meredith could feel the heat coursing through her with the rough touch of her Master's ex-wife. Much as she had been taught to do in lap-dancing for her Master's male friends, Meredith leaned forward and ground her body rhythmically against Yvanna's, working her hips back and forth. They moved effortlessly, the many hours of exercise having rendered Meredith a lithe and capable sexual athlete.

Meredith began to rock back and forth harder, pumping her hips in just the way her Master liked her to fuck herself onto him. She felt her pussy flooding uncontrollably in trained response to the motion, her copious juices soaking through and spilling over the tiny lace thong in an instant. Droplets of her juice dampened Yvanna's dress. Yvanna firmly repositioned the hapless girl to face her now, and chuckled as Meredith rubbed her breasts in the older woman's face. She reached to curve her arm around Meredith's thigh, pulling the younger woman firmly against her. Her hand found Meredith's cunt, plucked the laughable covering of the lace thong out of the way, and began to stroke it again, more firmly this time, rubbing Meredith's slit and occasionally plunging two fingers inside. Now moaning openly, Meredith fucked herself onto Yvanna's hand, pulsing eagerly toward orgasm.

"Kiss me," said Yvanna. "Let's see if he's pierced that tongue of yours yet."

Meredith felt a shiver go through her at the use of that word "yet"—her tongue had not been pierced.

"Please, dear," said Phillip from behind Meredith. "You're giving away all my tricks."

"It's all right, darling," said Yvanna. "I've got a few tricks of my own. Now kiss me, Meredith, the way a woman likes it."

She felt her nervousness growing as she leaned her elbows on the back of the sofa; how *did* a woman like to be kissed? Meredith herself mostly liked to be held down, hair tangled in her Master's fingers and her face and buttocks rosy and tingling from an hour or more of firm slaps, as her mouth was forced open and savaged by the fiercely-thrusting heat of her Master's tongue. But she suspected that most women, perhaps Yvanna included, wanted a gentler, more tender kiss, and so that was what Meredith gave her, nervously and tentatively pecking her before pressing her mouth against the older woman's hungrily. But when her tongue slid gently into Yvanna's mouth she felt an unexpected rush of excitement that both confused and aroused her, sending an uncontrollable wave of hunger through her cunt.

It took her a moment of deep kissing to recognize what was having such an effect on her.

Yvanna's mouth tasted like Phillip's cock.

The taste was overwhelming, and unmistakable; Meredith had swallowed her Master's organ enough times to know every nuance of that rich, musky taste. But not just his cock was there; Meredith could also taste, mingled with it, the taste of his come. Her Master had come in Yvanna's mouth.

Meredith almost pulled back, even as arousal ferociously took her over. But by that time, Phillip had come behind her, and his fingers snaked into her hair, holding her in place as Meredith's mouth was eagerly taken by Yvanna's thrusting tongue. Phillip held her there as his hand traveled up her thighs; hungrily, without even knowing she was doing it, Meredith pushed herself onto his hand when he touched her cunt. Two fingers slid into her easily, and Meredith began to work her hips again, this time even more eagerly than before.

She was wet. Unaccountably wet. Juice dripped down onto her Master's fingers and rivulets of it baptized her thighs. Meredith fucked herself desperately onto her Master's hand, even as the hot flame of jealousy exploded in her. *She sucked his cock*, she thought as Yvanna kissed her. *She sucked my lover's cock.*

But Meredith knew she had long since abandoned any claim she might have had on Phillip's sexual pleasures. She had given him unquestioning obedience—and he had chosen to dally with this woman. Meredith, then, would dally with her too, as she was being ordered to do.

She would make love with Yvanna, with the woman who had just been taken by her Master. She would service the woman, for her Master's pleasure.

"Mmmmm," cooed Yvanna when Phillip let Meredith go. "She tastes almost as good as you do. And quite an eager little kisser. I wonder if she'll like the taste of me on your cock as much as she likes the taste of you in my mouth."

Again, Meredith's stomach churned as jealousy flashed through her, but she let the fear and envy drain away as she felt Yvanna's hands touching her breasts, pinching the hard nipples, and Phillip began to finger-fuck her. Meredith's hips worked fervently, pushing her cunt onto first two, then three of her Master's fingers as Yvanna pulled her upper body forward and began to suckle Meredith's tiny tits.

"She's got me wet as a schoolgirl," gasped Yvanna. "Do something about that, will you, Phillip? You know what a girl likes. You've seen to it so many times yourself; I'm sure Meredith will get the hang of it quickly."

Meredith's head swam as Phillip gently eased her off the couch, pushing her head between his ex-wife's thighs as Yvanna swept the insubstantial fabric of her dress out of the way. There, fully revealed, was a smooth-shaved and unpierced pussy, glistening with juice. Clearly, Yvanna *still* didn't wear panties.

Phillip's hand, firmly holding Meredith's hair, pushed

her face between the older woman's thighs as Yvanna slid her ass forward to the edge of the white sofa. Before Meredith even had a chance to think about it, she was licking.

She almost expected the taste that greeted her—the taste of Phillip's pleasure, the sticky aromatic juice that told Meredith her Master had not only made love with this woman, but had done it *twice*—at least—and had been brought to completion by the shaved pussy that Meredith was now expected to service. And yet, when she did feel the thick jizz leaking onto her tongue, she felt another surge of jealousy— but by then, her Master's hand was so firmly in her hair that she could not have pulled back if she had wanted to.

And she didn't want to. Blessed with the taste of her Master's come, even leaking out of this hussy's cunt, Meredith eagerly began to worship, suckling at Yvanna's clit and licking down to her tight opening. Yvanna moaned softly; when it became quite clear that Meredith was going to not grudgingly, not just willingly but *enthusiastically* service the older woman, Phillip released his grip on Meredith's hair and firmly grasped her thighs. Meredith moved to open her legs, obediently, as she had been taught to do whenever her Master touched her there. But before she could even do that, Phillip had forced them open and tugged the crotch of her thong well to the side.

The distant rattle of her Master's belt buckle sent a sudden thrill through Meredith; it made her dizzy with excitement to know that even after pleasuring himself with this woman twice, he could still get it up for her. There was only an instant for her to think about that before the thick head of her Master's cock violated her, big enough to stretch her open painfully in the first instant of penetration even *after* she had been opened up first by two of Yvanna's slender fingers and then by three of Phillip's thick ones. But the flood of juice that met the Master's cock as he sank into her slicked the way so amply that by the time Meredith was thrusting herself violently onto Phillip's cock, only cascading waves of pleasure were exploding through her near-naked body. She devoured Yvanna's cunt with newfound fervor as the older woman moaned and cried out, seizing Meredith's head with both hands to force the girl's eagerly suckling mouth more firmly against her shaved cunt. The feel of that possessive gesture was what finally drove Meredith over the edge into an intense orgasm, and her tongue only worked faster as ecstasy flooded through her. Her hips, too, picked up force, pounding her cunt so hard onto Phillip's cock that he grabbed her hips and forced her to hold still while he ravaged her—ten thrusts, twenty, thirty, while Meredith continued to come, soaring high on her orgasm even as her swift tongue brought Yvanna off—and then Phillip let himself go deep inside her, inundating Meredith's cunt with the same blessed issue that had so flavored Yvanna's.

Whimpering hungrily, Meredith continued to lick even as Yvanna reclined on the sofa, practically hanging off of it. The older woman thrashed back and forth, moaning loudly as Meredith serviced her too-sensitive pussy. Finally, Yvanna pushed Meredith off, and the young blonde looked up panting, her mouth and chin running with the thick juices of Yvanna's cunt and the pungent savor of Phillip's come.

"Not bad," said Yvanna breathlessly. "She's taken to it quickly. Phillip, I think she'll learn to become quite a little cunt-licker before the wedding, don't you?"

Behind Meredith, Phillip chuckled. He leaned over

his slave, pressing her into the sofa as he kissed his ex-wife tenderly.

"She'd better," said Phillip when his lips left Yvanna's. "You remember which wife Yvanna is, don't you, Meredith?"

Her face cradled in Yvanna's lap, Meredith said softly:

"Yes, Sir. She's your fourth wife."

"I thought we'd work backward," said Phillip cheerfully. "Antonia's flying in next week."

"Mmmm," cooed Yvanna. "She's the one with those fantastic tits, isn't she?"

"That's right," said Phillip.

Yvanna laughed lightly. "I don't have to be back in Paris until the fifteenth. I think I'll stay for that. Unless it's an imposition, Phillip?"

"Not at all, my dear," said Phillip. "Meredith, you'll be happy to keep our guest entertained while she's here, won't you?"

Meredith affectionately kissed Yvanna's ivory thigh, her blood quickening at the scent of her Master's pleasure still wafting from deep inside.

"Yes, Sir," she said breathlessly.

Yvanna caressed Meredith's face and stroked her hair with her long, thin fingers.

"It's so sweet of you to let me try out your fiancée, darling," said Yvanna to Phillip. "She definitely passes the test."

Nine Ball, Corner Pocket

Michelle Houston

Jesse leaned against the wall, his legs crossed at the ankle. A cue stood to attention in front of his groin, gripped between strong, folded arms. Across the pool table, Rhiannon leaned down and lined up her shot. The tip of her tongue licked between her lips as she concentrated.

"Two ball to the nine, corner pocket," she said.

Jesse shot a quick glance at the table before giving a soft, derisive snort.

Glaring, Rhiannon's gaze lifted to his. "Don't think I can make it?"

"Not a chance, honey," was his self-satisfied response.

"Oh really?" She pulled away from the table, striking her "I can't believe you're doubting me" stance.

Jesse snorted again. He was accustomed to her moods and poses. When it came to pool, he was also familiar with her abilities, or rather, lack of them. After all, they'd played many similar games here at his home, on the same table. They'd also played a different kind of sport, fucking each other senseless on its emerald-green velvet. He could almost hear the tiny whimpers in her throat as she climaxed, her sweet juices running down her legs as he pounded into her from behind.

"Care to make a wager on that?" she snapped, interrupting his sordid thoughts.

Jesse started, realizing he hadn't heard what she'd said. He asked her to repeat herself. When she did, he grinned. "Rhiannon, I'm not going to take your money."

"I wasn't talking about money, darlin'. I meant something more wicked." As she spoke, her eyes danced with mischief.

Intrigued, he pushed off from the wall and stepped toward the pool table. Leaning on the rail, he asked, "How wicked?"

"Mmmm," she purred, licking her lips. "How about, if I miss this shot, you get to fuck my tight little ass?"

Straining to think straight at her announcement, Jesse wondered what the catch was. "And if you make the shot?" came his faintly suspicious reply.

Quick as a whip, she retorted, "I get to watch you get your tight little ass fucked." Her voice was full of amusement.

Bingo, there was the catch, although somehow, it didn't seem like such a bad trade. Rhiannon had been hinting about wanting to watch him and another man for a while, ever since he'd confessed his interest in gay porn. Her idea contained a certain dark appeal.

Before he lost his nerve, he agreed to her sinful dare. "You're on babe, but on one condition: if you win I still get to fuck your tight little ass. Just the way you've always wanted. You can't fool me, I know you're dying for it."

He was tempted to startle her with a sudden noise, but the glare Rhiannon shot his way stopped him. Sometimes it sucked to be with someone so long that they knew you well enough to predict your next move. But on reflection, given the killer blow job Rhiannon had given him the night before, it was a welcome trade-off with also having that person know your personal hot spots.

The tip of her tongue was back between her lips again, causing him to squirm as it drew his attention there. The way she was stroking the pool stick wasn't helping his peace of mind either.

Drawing the cue back, she slid it slowly forward again, almost tapping the cue ball. Jesse's attention was further divided as she widened her stance, took a deep breath, and slowly swung her arm back.

As the cue slid forward between her fingers, Jesse held his breath. Regardless of the outcome, they both knew Rhiannon's ass would no longer be virgin territory, but he wasn't so certain about his. As much as he worried, he found himself hoping she made the shot.

The two ball gently tapped the nine and for a moment, it hugged the rim, before falling into the pocket. In that moment, Jesse knew Rhiannon had triumphed. He only hoped that in the end, he'd win as well. After her victory, Rhiannon planted a quick kiss on Jesse's lips and then headed home for the night, leaving him to dwell on what was to come.

Jesse brooded over his position for the next several days, sitting in front of the TV, intently watching several rented videos showing gay men in various erotic situations. Each afternoon he rushed home from work, first checking his answering machine, before playing a video and lubricating his hands.

He masturbated to scenes of construction workers, college roommates, and military men, but his favorite movie featured two men in a pool hall. He stroked his cock raw as he repeatedly watched one man bugger the other with the butt end of a pool cue, before the cue wielder fucked his willing victim.

It gave Jesse an added thrill when he pressed a finger inside his ass, wriggling it as he jerked himself off. He'd even been tempted to try something a bit firmer and bigger, like the mini-vibrator Rhiannon kept in the nightstand, but he hadn't been able to work up the nerve.

As evening fell on the third day, Jesse heard his cell phone ring and he glanced at the display. Rhiannon had finally decided to call. As he answered, loud techno-music assaulted his ears. He could barely hear Rhiannon's shouts, but eventually he made out what she was saying.

"I'll be at your place in about an hour. Wear those jeans of yours I like and nothing else, and darlin'—make sure you have the lube and a few condoms handy—I'm bringing a friend."

A click sounded in his ear as the loud music and Rhiannon's voice were replaced by a dial tone. His hand suddenly shaking, Jesse hung up the phone and then rushed to pick up the clutter in his apartment before company arrived.

An hour later, he'd just finished clearing the mess when the doorbell rang.

Closing the dishwasher and flicking the switch, he

surveyed the apartment as he headed to the front door. The rented videos were hidden, the couch cushions were flipped over and he'd moved the lube into the bedroom. The tube now sat on the dresser, next to a full box of condoms. Everything looked normal, except he was wearing jeans that were slightly baggy over his hips, no boxers, no shirt—and he was about to have sex with a man he'd never met.

Forcing a smile to his lips, he concentrated on steadying his hand; first one deep breath, then another. Closing his eyes, he pictured Rhiannon leaning over the pool table, her legs spread and her asshole lubed and ready. Glancing at his hand again, he noticed it was steady, but he also caught sight of the increasing bulge in his jeans. With a nervous flourish, Jesse opened the door to the wonders that were to come.

Jesse's eyes trailed over Rhiannon's "friend" as he pondered why he looked so familiar. It only took a moment for him to realize he knew Neil, though normally Rhiannon's editor was dressed in a nice suit and sported slicked-back hair. He oozed heterosexual vibes and turned many a feminine head.

Yet now, the man standing in front of him was rugged, dressed in tight jeans and a white T-shirt. His tattoos were clearly visible and a very noticeable hard-on strained against the seam of his jeans.

"Jesse, I hear I get to pop your cherry," Neil taunted. He placed a hand against Jesse's chest and gently pushed him back into the apartment. Slowly sliding his hand down his willing victim's torso to the waist of his jeans, he hooked his finger in a belt loop and pulled the unresisting man towards him.

Rhiannon closed the door behind them.

"Between you and me, I think I'm going to love every

minute of it. I have a feeling you will as well." Neil's words contained an almost addictive seductiveness.

Jesse gulped silently and opened his mouth to respond, but he never got a chance. Neil leaned forward and pressed his lips to his, sparking sudden feral desire. Almost instantly, Jesse felt his cock stiffen further. Unfulfilled fantasies roared through his mind. The texture of those male lips was similar to Rhiannon's, but different somehow. They were firmer and more impatient.

Neil took possession of Jesse's mouth, thrusting his tongue past parted lips. The insistent organ searched out its wet and warm opposite number. Neil's hands slid around Jesse's hips, pulling the shell-shocked man against him.

Jesse admired this display of dominance, even as he submitted. Groin to groin with the other man now, Jesse ground his hips slowly, igniting a trail of need in them both.

It turned him on all the more knowing that Rhiannon watched him and her best friend duel for control.

Jesse saw Neil pull back to look at him, and he knew what Neil would see because Rhiannon had told him often enough. Neil would notice the way his hair spiked slightly; he'd notice a crescent of thick lashes lying against dark cheeks. Jesse understood his own qualities, the perfect working-class construction worker, toned, tanned, and sexy as hell. Judging by the equally intoxicating looks of his partner, it was, he guessed, going to be a wild ride for them all.

As Jesse's eyes locked on Neil's, his seducer leaned down and kissed him again. At that moment, Jesse noticed the light floral scent of Rhiannon's perfume. She'd moved to stand beside him. He felt her carefully grasp his hand.

Half-directing, half-pulling, Rhiannon led the two men to the bedroom. Jesse allowed himself to be guided backward, to let Rhiannon and Neil set the pace. It was kind of nice to have the decision and details taken out of his hands.

As the door closed with a soft click, Jesse pulled away from Neil. For a second, the sensual haze cleared from his mind and the true reality of his situation dawned. Panic began to creep in.

"I can't do this," he whispered, his eyes darting to Rhiannon in a mute plea.

"Shhh baby," she whispered, stepping between the two men. Raising her hands to Jesse's chest, she also nodded slightly toward Neil, before turning back to reassure her boyfriend, "Nothing's going to happen that you don't want."

Slowly twining her fingers in the soft golden curls covering her lover's chest, she coaxed his lips down to hers. They kissed passionately, as her hands roamed over his ribs, down to the well-worn fly of his Levis. Undoing the buttons, she slipped his jeans over his ass and gravity took its effect.

Jesse watched as she kneeled down in front of him and lifted his feet, one after the other, until he'd stepped out of the worn, blue garment. "Just relax, baby, and let me take care of you," she said as she straightened up a little and met his gaze.

With a quick flick of her tongue to dampen her lips, she leaned forward slightly and kissed the head of his cock. A small drop of precum oozed from the tip and she teased him, swirling her tongue over the glistening drop, before sucking his length into her mouth. She tasted an inch, then pulled back, each delay driving him wild. Another inch, then again she backed off.

Slowly, sensually, she aroused him to a fever pitch. His hands twisted in her perfectly done hair, pulling the pins free and leaving her long tresses dangling down her back. Soon, he forgot all about the other man in the room, watching his beautiful siren have her way with his willing flesh.

Her hands tenderly cupped his ballsack, playing gently with the sensitive skin. Moaning softly, he arched into her mouth, thrusting his cock in a steady rhythm. Muted sucking sounds filled the room, his groans a low accompaniment.

As Rhiannon pulled back, he could hear the sound of her mouth on his flesh and his eyes flickered open. He saw Neil standing to his left, naked. A number of tattoos covered his tanned flesh. Then Neil's ink-black eyes met his and Jesse couldn't look away, even when Rhiannon's satiny mouth returned to his straining erection.

He watched, fascinated, as Neil cupped his own cock and gently stroked himself. Jesse desperately wanted to feel it pound into and stretch him to his limits. Then Rhiannon's mouth drove him back to the brink, before she suddenly pulled away again.

Now, he watched as her lovely lips closed around Neil's cock, sucking it deep within her warm, velvety mouth. Jealousy pulsed inside him as he gazed, but not of the sort he'd expected. He wanted to taste Neil's flesh as well.

Dropping to his knees, he gently pushed Rhiannon away and moved to take her place. Hesitantly, he kissed Neil's stiffness, tasting the salty essence leaking from the bulging tip. Taking a deep breath, he opened his lips and sucked the inviting phallus deep into his mouth. He gagged, then backed off for a moment, remembering past girlfriends and their tentative attempts. Trying again, he took Neil's erection more deeply into his mouth.

Softly, Neil's hands came to rest on Jesse's head, guiding him without pressure until he found a comfortable rhythm.

Jesse's eyes now focused completely on Neil, watching for subtle clues. He wasn't sure what to do next. When Neil's lids fluttered closed, and his Adam's apple bobbed, Jesse knew he was doing okay. Filled with confidence, he sucked harder, stroking his hands up and down Neil's thighs, enjoying the feel of the wiry hair beneath his palms.

Jesse knew Neil was close to orgasm when he felt his hands tighten in his hair. He knew because when Rhiannon went down on him, he reacted the same way, holding her face still as he fucked her throat.

Jesse watched as Neil's eyes opened suddenly and his nostrils flared a little. Then, out of the corner of his eye, he saw what had drawn Neil's attention away. Rhiannon was slowly undressing, her hands running over her stomach and thighs, caressing her smooth skin. For a moment, his hands itched to return to his sweet love's softness, but as drops of precum leaked from Neil's slit, he returned his attention to his male paramour.

Only her heels, hose, and garter remained as Rhiannon knelt next to Jesse. Carefully lying on her stomach, she shifted as close to him as possible and then softly parted his ass cheeks, sliding her tongue along the cleft. Jesse trembled as she rimmed him, her tongue slipping past his ass-ring. Many times before he had tasted her forbidden crevice, sampling the tangy, sweaty flesh, imagining it being done to him, but he had never been able to ask for it.

Jesse could feel Neil's gaze on him as he experienced this delight for the first time.

Jesse felt Rhiannon pull her tongue from his ass, giving the crevice one last deep lick before moving away. Sucking Neil's cock deep, he focused his attention solely on the taste and sensation of the velvety flesh in his mouth. A whisper of sound behind him barely gave him warning before Rhiannon pressed a finger against his sphincter and pushed.

He jerked in response. Instantly, Neil was soothing him—tenderly brushing his hands over his face and shoulders. He quickly guided Jesse back into a steady rhythm, as Rhiannon's finger slipped deeper, and was joined by another, provoking a curious tingling.

Minutes passed as the three reveled in their exploration. Then Rhiannon pulled away from Jesse and stood. Stepping between the two men, she moved toward the bedside table and grabbed the tube of lubricant, squeezing some into her palm.

She rubbed her hands together before carefully spreading it between her buttocks. She forced a finger inside her anus and wiggled her hand. Jesse swallowed as his eyes almost crossed. He swallowed a hint of panic, watching Neil move to stand behind her.

She slipped her finger free and held her ass cheeks apart as Neil thrust his lube-coated digits deep into her ass. With his other hand, he guided her onto her belly across the bed, her feet planted firmly on the floor.

Jesse watched as Neil forced his fingers in and out of her butt, gently twisting them as he did. He was intrigued by the look on his lover's face, as her ass fought a bit against the invasion. Small streams of fire flooded his body, his cock hard and throbbing as he imagined his own fingers up Rhiannon's ass, while Neil manipulated his virgin sphincter.

"Spread your legs further," Neil demanded, as he settled his body between her silky thighs. His palm firmly planted against her back, he pinned her legs against the bed with his, and continued to fuck her with his fingers. The fire that raced through Jesse soon turned into an inferno, as Rhiannon responded to the sensual invasion, arching her hips, guiding Neil deeper.

She lifted her body from the bed, and moved her hand down to her clit. Jesse moved closer, his emotions whirling as his hands stroked his cock of their own volition.

Fisting his cock, Jesse watched as Rhiannon bucked against Neil, timing her finger thrusts to his until, together, they fucked her into a quivering orgasm.

It was a breathtaking sight. In that moment, seeing the satisfied look on his girlfriend's face, he knew he was making the right choice. Neil was patient, tender, and obviously skilled.

In a moment of brazenness, Jesse knelt on the bed next to Rhiannon, reached back, and parted his own asscheeks. His gaze locked on Rhiannon's and, nervous as hell, he attempted a smile. He wasn't certain how successful he was.

Jesse couldn't quite believe he'd parted his own ass cheeks, but as Neil moved behind him and slid the tip of the lubricant tube into his ass, he no longer cared. His body demanded satisfaction, even as his mind rebelled. He knew there would be discomfort and maybe even pain.

Watching Rhiannon's face had underlined that fact. He knew her well enough to know she'd tried to hide it. He also knew he had nerves in that sensitive area that a woman didn't. If Rhiannon had adjusted, and even enjoyed it, he could only imagine what he would feel.

And he was tired of waiting, wondering what it would be like. Living with the constant craving.

Taking a deep breath, he tried to prepare for the sensation of a handful of cool gel around his ass. When he experienced it, he trembled as he anticipated what was to follow.

He sensed Neil shift away, and he turned his head when he heard foil rustling. He saw Neil standing next to Rhiannon; she was sliding a condom over his weeping cock. Other than the sweet spread of Rhiannon's pussy lips, he wondered if he'd ever seen a more erotic sight. Her dainty hands slid over the latex-coated flesh, spreading a layer of lube over Neil's eager erection. Her eyes met Jesse's, and she smiled her gentle siren's smile.

Unable to stand the suspense, he closed his eyes and clenched the sheets. The feel of gentle hands on his ass made him tremble. Neil moved to stand against him, reminiscent of the way he'd pinned Rhiannon down. A palm pressed against his back and Jesse took a deep breath.

"Relax." Neil's cultured tones contrasted sharply with the motifs that decorated his body. For a moment, Jesse wondered what had motivated Neil. He'd been tattooed at least six different times.

Relaxing, as a fingernail tapped against his anus, Jesse took a deep breath. Then, a long finger slipped past his ring. Soon, it was joined by a second. Slowly, they worked in and out of his ass, pushing against the ring of nerves. Twitching slightly, Jesse arched back into the touch.

It was like nothing he'd ever felt before. He had always been tempted to include ass play in his sex life, but before Rhiannon, no other woman had been interested. Rhiannon was willing to fuck his ass with a strap-on, but first, she wanted him to be fully breached by a man. With that lucky pool shot, she'd made her requirement a reality, and fulfilled a fantasy for them both.

Lost in the sensations, with sparks of pleasure racing throughout his body, he didn't at first notice the pressure had eased. The first touch of Neil's cock against his ass-ring quickly brought his attention back to the present. Trying to relax was hard.

"Wait a moment, Neil." Rhiannon's soft voice stilled the pressure against Jesse's ass. Opening his eyes, Jesse watched Rhiannon settle in front of him. She knelt, with her legs parted. Reaching down, she separated her slick pussy lips.

Dipping her fingers deeply, she coated them in her juices and spread the smooth essence of her arousal on Jesse's lips. Licking the sweetness, he closed his eyes and savored the moment.

Distracted, he didn't notice Neil pressing against his ring again until Neil's glans had slipped inside him. A moment passed, and he felt a curious stretching sensation as Neil's cock completely penetrated his ass. Gritting his teeth, he waited for the pain, but there wasn't much. As Neil moved within him, Jesse's fists gripped the sheets and he followed his lover's rhythm. Within moments, they were working together in a steady thrust, then withdrawal.

His ass full of cock for the first time, Jesse watched as Rhiannon thrust two fingers deep into her pussy, her other hand playing with her clit. Both hands soon grew wet with her juices, as she fucked herself into another orgasm. The scent of her arousal flooded his senses.

Clenching at each of Neil's thrusts, Jesse ground his hips against the bed. His cock steadily leaked precum and his balls tightened. Jesse knew it was all about to end. He was about to orgasm with a man's cock sawing in and out of his ass. With each thrust, his erection rubbed against the soft sheets. With each withdrawal, his ass ached for more.

Thrust and withdraw; grind and clench. Over and over, the two lovers worked against, then with each other, drawing both of them closer to the inevitable.

Animalistic grunts echoed off the walls, but Jesse was too far gone to notice the sounds were coming from his own mouth.

His ass begged for each hard thrust and his cock pulsed with need. Balls tight, he ground his hips as Neil pushed deep inside him. Clenching his lover tightly, he locked his legs and jerked spasmodically. Weird sensations wracked his body as he climaxed. Hot, sticky squirts shot from his throbbing flesh, creating a warm, tacky pool on the bed. Convulsing with each spurt of his orgasm, he clenched tighter, pulling Neil into the vortex.

Closing his eyes, Jesse arched against Neil as his new lover pounded into him. Within moments, Neil's slight weight collapsed onto Jesse's back. Vaguely, Jesse heard Rhiannon gasp as she climaxed a third time, but he was too lost in new sensations to care. All that mattered was the steadily softening cock in his ass, the weight of a man lying on him, and the come leaking from his own cock.

With a soft sigh he shifted, forcing Neil to roll off. With sleepy eyes, he watched as Neil pulled the latex from his cock, and tossed it in the trash. Jesse slid toward Rhiannon, making room for Neil on the bed. Pressing his face against Rhiannon's moist flesh, Jesse took a deep breath, as he struggled to bring sanity to a world made up entirely of tingling nerves.

"Mmmmm," he managed, as Rhiannon nuzzled her pussy against his lips.

Tentatively, he stuck his tongue out and wiggled it, as she ground against him. Her fingers occasionally brushed against his forehead. As he gradually collected his thoughts, his limbs still deliciously lethargic, Jesse rolled over just enough for Rhiannon to mount his face and grind herself to another screaming orgasm.

The bed dipped as Neil settled beside him, and Jesse shifted in response, spooning with his new lover. Within moments, Rhiannon had joined them, snuggling her back against Jesse's chest.

Lying there, the three held each other as they adjusted to the changes one night had caused. Jesse wasn't certain how Neil was going to fit into their relationship, but the fact Rhiannon had chosen him, instead of any number of bi and gay men she knew, spoke volumes. He knew Rhiannon had been attracted to her editor since day one, and that despite their attraction, they had become good friends.

Jesse felt Neil press a soft kiss against his neck, warm breath tickling his sweaty skin.

"You know she set you up, right?"

Neil's voice startled Jesse for a moment as he floated in a haze of contentment. Shifting himself and Rhiannon so that he could see both their faces, Jesse asked, "What do you mean?"

"I've been working with her for the last six weeks, teaching her to play pool. She used to suck, but lately, she's gotten rather good."

Jesse met Rhiannon's troubled gaze. He wanted to be upset that she had manipulated things, but he knew that would be unfair. She had given him something that they both wanted, but he hadn't been able to ask for. With that winning shot, she had freed him to fully enjoy his sexuality.

Leaning down, he pressed his lips to hers, hoping she could tell all the things he wanted to say, but couldn't.

Behind him, Neil shifted until his lips touched the lobe of Jesse's left ear. "And over the last six weeks, we've made a lot of plans for both of your tight asses. Tomorrow, all three of us are going to play nine ball, and winner fucks both losers."

Two Guys and a Girl
THOMAS S. ROCHE

The lobby didn't smell half as bad as Naomi expected. In fact, it smelled better than the alley it was located on, and in comparison it seemed almost clean. She had never been inside a porn theater, but she'd heard all the stories—feet sticking to the floor, rats the size of cats, that sort of thing. This wasn't any worse than a really bad locker room—which is not to say it smelled good, but it could conceivably be tolerable.

She took a deep breath to make sure the faint smell of bleach, come, and sweat wouldn't set off her allergies, and instead of sneezing she felt a vague surge in her pussy, repulsion mixed with attraction, fascination for all that male sweat and semen—as if it spelled a chemical formula—working its exotic magic on her curiosity. She looked up at the smudged glass box with a chaser light running sprints around the movie poster for *Two Guys and a Girl*, one of those porn-movie takeoffs on a Hollywood gig, some chick who looked very vaguely like Heather Graham between a dark-haired guy and a blond-haired guy, looking sleazy in pink spandex and go-go boots, the three of them obviously about to get it on. Naomi decided she'd stay.

The ticket counter was just inside the door. The guy took Naomi's money and she caught him doing a double take. She stared him down and he stared back, then smiled faintly before looking down. Naomi couldn't tell if he'd made her, seen beyond the hooded sweatshirt, slim build and faked gruff voice, or if he was just a guy cruising another guy. He was an older black man, good-looking and built. She smiled back at him, wondering if her smile looked enough like a guy's.

She took the ticket and sauntered slowly past the display case of off-pink dildos, ball gags, and penis pumps, noting that a thin layer of dust covered them.

Inside the theater was where the smell hit her, stronger than the lobby, intense. She had fantasized about that smell ever since the first time she'd heard somebody complain about it. She wasn't entirely sure what the fascination was, but it had nagged at her for what seemed like forever. She savored it, grossed out and turned-on at the same time.

There were only two guys, both of them down toward the front. *Two guys and a girl,* Naomi thought. *If they only knew.* Neither guy turned around as she entered. Naomi took a seat in the third row from the back and watched the credits roll, suppressing a need to laugh at the stupid performer names. Then the action started, a badly lit scene of a garishly made-up blonde woman giving head to a Latino guy with an enormous cock. Naomi felt a pulse between her legs and all of a sudden she really, really wanted to masturbate. She fought the urge for about two minutes while the blow job continued, but when the Latino guy started holding the blonde's head she gave up. She cocked her body to one side and slipped her hand down her sweat pants.

She had no idea she would come that fast. She never had before, not like that, not explosively, eyes wide, staring, trying to suppress the yelp that wanted to explode from her lips. She came for a long time, one of those orgasms that surges through you to the point where about ten percent of you is waiting to see when it stops and the rest of you is begging for it to go on forever. She was right in the middle of that when two more guys walked in. They sat down right behind her. She didn't dare turn around. But she realized almost immediately that she could smell them, their musky bodies mixed with the harsh scent of the theater.

She couldn't take her hand out of her pants; that would be way too obvious. The telltale motion of her arm would no doubt give her away. The best she could do was curl up a little and pull the bottom of her sweatshirt over her arm, and pray they didn't notice that her hand was jammed down her pants. The aftereffects of her orgasm were still pulsing through her. She felt her muscles contracting deep inside, felt her fingers still jammed against her clit. She was so distracted by her own pleasure and the fear that she would be discovered that it took her a long minute to recognize the sound behind her.

The two guys were kissing.

At first she thought there was a blow job involved, but something told her it was a kiss. She fought the urge to turn around and look, and when she heard the sound of a belt being undone it did not get any easier to keep staring forward at the screen. Two women were making love, kissing with mock hunger as their hands explored each other's crotches. Naomi had never kissed a woman, and she certainly had never had two guys kissing so close to her. The screen blurred into nothing as she heard someone's zipper go down. She wasn't sure when her hand started to move again, but it did. Her clit was so swollen and raw from her intense orgasm that it hurt to rub it. That didn't stop her; nor did the sound of one guy sliding to his knees, the feel of her theater seat rocking as he crammed himself into the space behind it, sucking the other guy's dick. She heard faint hypermasculine grunts, mingling with the girl-moans from the movie.

Naomi rubbed gingerly, her heart pounding as she felt another orgasm approaching. She knew she shouldn't come again; this was going way further than she'd meant to. But before she could come, she heard the creak of the chairs as the guy leaned forward, his hot breath on the back of her neck.

"Want a blow job?" he asked.

She moved like an automaton, driven by the throb in her loins. She turned her head, cocked it slightly, and said in as gruff a voice as she could manage: "Nah, but I'll suck your friend."

What the fuck was she doing? Sure, she'd crammed a condom into her pocket—why, she hadn't known at the time, she just figured it might be nice to have. But suck off a strange fag in a porn theater? That was going way further than just wanking to a fuck film. That was going too far, way too far.

"Yeah, all right," the guy said.

Naomi kept her face averted as she came around the end of the aisle. She pulled the hood of her sweatshirt down and moved toward them. The guy on his knees got into the seat, not looking at Naomi, and hunched over awkwardly so he could keep sucking as the other guy undid his friend's belt and zipper, pulled out his cock. Breathing hard, Naomi took the seat next to him. The first guy tried to look her in the eyes. She kept looking down, at the anonymous hard cock jutting out of the guy's pants. She ripped the condom open, popped it in her mouth. Thank God she'd practiced this trick on her last boyfriend. But this time her mouth was watering so much that it was really hard to do it. By the time she had the condom on him, there was drool everywhere. She started to suck his cock, feeling her pussy juice flowing as she did. She was still very close to orgasm, but of course touching herself was out of the question now. Wasn't it?

She glanced up and saw the upright guy's eyes flashing as he looked at her intensely. It was dark, very dark. Naomi slid her hand down her pants and touched her clit, desperately trying to make her hand look like it was moving up and down on her cock. She kept sucking the anonymous cock as she stroked herself, feeling her pussy juice around her fingers. As she mounted toward her second orgasm, she felt the guy she was sucking put his hand on her head and lift his hips off the seat. She switched hands so she could stroke him off, driving him toward his orgasm while she awkwardly crammed her left hand into her pants and pushed herself toward hers. Then the guy was coming, his cock spasming inside the condom, Naomi wishing she could taste his come coursing into her mouth—and that thought bringing her orgasm on like a flash of fire, as she kept sucking through the guy's groans and bucking hip-thrusts while he pumped his friend's unsheathed dick with his hand.

As soon as the guy was finished coming, he bent down

and started sucking his friend's dick again. Naomi stayed bent over as she felt him taking her hand, pulling it over, wrapping it around the still-hard dick so she could jerk it off into the his mouth. There were more moans, a naked cock pulsing in her hand, a mouth sucking and gulping come. As the cock softened in her hand, she realized there were dribbles of come running over her fingers. It took her a minute to realize what was happening; she felt the tongue working around her fingers, hungry lips closing around them. Then she felt the guy freeze. He pulled Naomi's hand out of his mouth, sitting bolt upright and staring at her wide-eyed, as she realized, all of a sudden: that was the hand she'd had in her pants until a moment ago. She barely even realized what was happening as the guy reached out and pushed back her hooded sweatshirt.

Naomi sat paralyzed, staring at the two guys. She wasn't sure what she saw in their eyes—fear, pleasure, revulsion, fascination?—and she didn't particularly care. Maybe she'd gone too far, maybe she hadn't. But she wasn't going any further.

As nonchalantly as possible, Naomi stood up and started walking up the row of chairs. The two guys just stared, following her every inch of the way as she reached the aisle and bolted for the door.

Once she got out into the alley, she took a deep breath, welcomed by the alley's smell of urine and garbage. She massaged her temples, realizing in a rush that the smear on her forehead was the stranger's come. She inhaled deeper, the mix of scents sending her head into a spin. Smiling to herself, she wiped her hand on the front of her sweatshirt and rushed down the alley toward the bus.

Circle of Friends
Rebecca Henderson

On the screen, six naked women slipped and writhed, their well-oiled limbs gliding around one another's bodies like snakes. Mouths and tongues licked and suckled breasts, feet, fingers, and pussies; fingers slid easily into cracks and crevices; limbs slid against swollen clits in an oily, slippery orgy of skin on skin.

Mara grimaced and turned away. It wasn't the pornography that bothered her—hell, she liked a good fuck flick as well as the next person—it was the thought of all that oil. *Ick!*

Apparently this was not an issue for her husband. Jim stood mesmerized in front of the fifty-four-inch screen. His mouth hung open and drool pooled in his lower lip. Mara loved her husband to death, but really, did he have to *drool* over the movie? Stealing a surreptitious glance around the room, however, Mara realized that his reactions were not that far removed from the rest of the ten or twelve other people there. Everyone sat watching the TV with expressions that varied from dazed to outright lustful. Mara shook her head and grinned to herself. She had a feeling one or more of the bedrooms in the house would soon be in use. This was a swingers' party, after all, and most of the people there could be expected to hook up with other partygoers at some point in the evening. The porn on the television was just one way to get everybody hot and ready to go.

Everyone except Mara. She seldom "hooked up" with anyone at these parties anyway, preferring to use the venue as a place to meet possible new lovers without actually embarking on a sexual liaison at the party itself. Jim was just the opposite: he liked the quick fuck in a back room, the more anonymous the better, sometimes more than one a night. It turned Mara on, the thought of him scoring with some strange woman in a back room, pushing her down face-first on the bed, raising her ass in the air and shoving his cock into a warm, wet, anonymous cunt, rutting blindly against her like an animal until he came. Just thinking about it now made Mara squirm a bit against the seat of the chair.

The sexual activity on the screen was reaching a crescendo, the penultimate act appearing to be a fisting in the middle of the oil pit where the women writhed against one another. One woman lay prone, her legs held open by two others, being fisted by a particularly busty brunette, while another sucked and twisted her nipples and the last woman rode her face, grinding her cunt against the fisted-one's mouth in a paroxysm of pleasure that Mara knew had to be faked.

Nothing could feel that good—and Mara'd had some good sex in her life.

Mara sighed and went into the kitchen. She knew most of the men at the party, and those that she didn't she wasn't particularly interested in getting to know. Perhaps she was becoming jaded with the whole swingers' scene. She still enjoyed the excitement of taking a new lover, but there didn't seem to be anyone new that could make her feel that excitement anymore. Maybe she needed to expand her circle of friends.

She heard a sound behind her and saw Beth, the party's hostess, come in. As always, Beth was dressed in the most outrageously sexy, naughty outfit. Tonight she wore an old-fashioned "June Cleaver"-type apron, high heels, frilly thong panties—and nothing else. Mara grinned at her and openly admired the other woman's lush, rounded curves and sexy outfit. She admired Beth's nerve in wearing whatever she wanted to as well. Even though Mara knew she had a lovely body, she had never been able to work up the courage to display herself that way. But then again, Beth was an exhibitionist, and oftentimes ended up being as much a part of the show as the porn movies were. Her semipublic sexcapades were much talked about and enjoyed in their circle.

"Not enjoying the movie, Mara?" Beth asked, as she went to the refrigerator and took out a premade pitcher of margaritas.

Mara leaned back against the counter and shook her head. "Not my scene, I guess."

Beth glanced over at her. "But I thought you liked porn...."

"It's not that," Mara said, shuddering again. "It's all that oil! Ewwww…"

Beth looked over at Mara in surprise, and then laughed. "You're not serious!"

"Sure I am…are you telling me you'd do that? Get in a pit full of oiled-up women?"

"Oh please!" Beth said. "That would be heaven! Where can I sign up?"

Mara laughed and shook her head. She also admired Beth's easy bisexuality, although she'd never tried to emulate it herself. It wasn't that she didn't find other women attractive— quite opposite, in fact—it was just that she'd never been brave enough to experiment that way.

Beth stepped closer to her, close enough that her full, heavy breasts pressed against Mara's smaller ones. Looking into Mara's eyes she grinned wickedly. "Are you telling me," she asked, her voice low and sexy as she leaned closer, "that you wouldn't love to slither and slide against me and four or five of our best girlfriends?" As she spoke she pressed herself fully against Mara and proceeded to slide up and down her suggestively, pressing in strategic places with her hip, thigh, and knee. "Imagine," she continued, her mouth a breath away from Mara's, "if we were doing this totally naked, skin to skin…"

Mara shuddered and couldn't help pressing back against her, feeling the slip of her silk dress against her skin and the heat of Beth's skin through it.

Beth laughed and pulled back. "And here I thought you were unabashedly hetero, Mara, dear," she said.

Mara took an unsteady breath and leaned back against the counter as she watched Beth return to her task of pouring margaritas. She'd thought so, too. She'd been completely unprepared for the flare of heat she'd felt when Beth had pushed against her, for the leap of desire as she'd felt Beth's skin slide against her own.

"I, um…," she began, but Beth laughed and cut her off.

"It's okay," she said. "Liking the feel of another person's body doesn't make you het or bi or gay. It's a natural response, like feeling good when someone hugs you. Like feeling good after a massage. Skin-to-skin contact is natural, honey, we all need it. Some of us—" she looked over her shoulder with raised eyebrows and a grin, "some of us even crave it. Maybe that's why everyone is so fascinated by the oil scenario, why it seems so sexy to us."

And then she left the kitchen with the pitcher and glasses. Mara watched her go with a mixture of excitement and disappointment. The moment was gone, she realized, when she could have told Beth of her secret fantasies, the ones in which she explored what it would be like to touch another woman, to kiss her, to taste her.

In the days following the party, Mara found herself thinking back to that moment in the kitchen over and over. What could she have done differently? Kissed Beth? But what if Beth hadn't been coming on to her, just teasing her? She just didn't know how this game was played. Where relationships and encounters with men were concerned, Mara knew her stuff, she played the game as well or better than most others; she had every confidence in herself. With women, though, she was out of her depth.

And then there were her dreams. Nightly, it seemed, she dreamed of the feel of skin on skin, of sliding and slipping against anonymous bodies...women's bodies, bodies that had been oiled until they gleamed.... She woke in a sweat every time, with her heart pounding and a throbbing between her legs that would not be denied. She'd never been squeamish about masturbating, but neither had she felt much need to. In the days after the party she found herself with her hands between her legs more times than she could count, an insistent throbbing desire there that she couldn't help but try to assuage. Jim finally woke up one night just as she brought herself to a powerful orgasm. He rolled over and touched her gently, then more urgently as he realized what she was doing, eventually pressing an enormous erection against her hip. Still pulsing with her orgasm she opened her legs to him and clutched him to her as he thrust into her with a groan. When he climaxed moments later she did too, crying out his name as she came.

"Wow," he said afterward, "what were *you* dreaming about?"

She laughed self-consciously and felt her face heat in the dark. "I don't know," she mumbled. He leaned up on his hands and looked down into her face.

"You're fibbing!" he said. "Why?"

She sighed. "I was dreaming about oiled-up women," she admitted.

He chuckled. "I knew you'd come around eventually."

"Just because I dreamed about it doesn't mean I want it," she retorted.

For her birthday, three days later, he gave her a gift certificate for a massage at a popular day spa in town. "Go on," he said. "See what it feels like." She rolled her eyes, but admitted to a bit of curiosity. She'd never had a massage.

Afterward she wondered how she'd gone so long before getting one. The feel of the masseuse's hands on her, the feel of the massage oil sliding over her body, was enough to drive her to distraction. Lying there on the bench, she wondered if the masseuse could smell her musky excitement—and then admitted that she didn't care, and gave herself over to the feelings and fantasies that the massage provoked. That night, after a particularly energetic round of lovemaking with Jim, she told him about her experience with Beth in the kitchen, and the conflicting feelings it had brought to the surface.

"Tell me what you fantasize might have happened, Mara," he said, his breath tickling the nape of her neck. "Talk to me…tell me what you wanted to happen." And while she did, he stroked her smooth, soft skin. As she began to get caught up in her fantasy, he slipped a finger inside her pussy lips and then took it out to stroke her juice between her thighs and over her clit. She caught her breath and pushed against his hand and he slid two fingers into her and then three, while she twisted against him and told him how she'd fantasized pulling aside Beth's apron and taking her heavy breasts into her hands, cupping and pulling on them, putting her mouth on them, sucking on them…

She gasped and stopped talking, unwilling to go on, but when she stopped so did his hand. "Keep talking," he demanded, his voice hoarse.

She moaned, thrusting against him, but he wouldn't start again and so she continued, her voice breathy and strained as she spoke. She imagined Beth pushing her against the counter and reaching up under her dress to pull her panties aside. She imagined Beth's fingers inside her, and the taste of her mouth and the feel of her friend's body against her own. She opened her legs completely and Jim shoved four fingers into her. She was so wet her juices dripped over and around his hand. She arched against him as he cupped his hand into a V and pushed it back inside her, thumb and all. And as he pushed as hard as he dared against her, into her, and she spread her legs as far as she could for him, she told him that she fantasized being the woman in the oil pit with another woman's hand up her cunt, fisting her. When she came it was like an explosion inside of her.

The next afternoon Beth called Mara and told her that she and Cecelia wanted to take her out to dinner for her birthday the following Saturday.

"Come over to my house," Beth told her, "and we'll take my car from here."

When Mara arrived at Beth's the house seemed unusually quiet, with only one light on in the back of the house. "Beth?" Mara called through the open front door, after no one answered her knock. There was still no answer, although she did hear voices from the direction of the back rooms. Following the voices back, she found herself in front of a closed door. The voices most definitely were coming from that room. Cautiously she turned the knob and pushed on the door.

It immediately swung open and a chorus of voices yelled, "Surprise!" Mara jumped back involuntarily with an exclamation that was cut off mid-squeal. For a moment she just stared at the vision in front of her, unable to believe what she was seeing.

"Beth? Cecelia…Joan! And Teresa? Oh my God, what are you guys…?" She stammered to a stop, unable to go on. To a woman, they were all naked and lounging in a rectangular plastic children's pool, the kind with the blow-up sides. And their bodies all glistened with oil.

Her friends laughed and jumped up to surround her. They pulled at her clothes, laughing and teasing her all the while, until she too was naked, in spite of her halfhearted protests. Before she knew what was happening they had pushed her back into the pool and surrounded her, their hands oily and soft on her skin as they smoothed a bottle of oil over her. At first she laughed self-consciously, but soon the laughter turned to something else, as hands touched her everywhere, as tongues and lips and teeth licked and bit, tasting her, inflaming her. She began to writhe and moan, unable to deny the desire that heated her, unable to keep her body from responding as she felt warm, wet fingers slide into her, opening her, stroking her. It hardly mattered, and she could hardly tell, whose hands were where and doing what. It all became a blur of pure sensation, her body became a throbbing point of heat and need. The feel of the other women's bodies on hers, touching hers, sliding against hers, soft and slick and sweet-smelling with the oil, was amazing, sensual in a way that she had never imagined.

Much later, wrapped in a thick terry-cloth robe, her skin washed clean but still soft and supple after the oil-bath, Mara lay back on the couch against Beth's knees. Looking around at her friends as they talked quietly and sipped glasses of wine, Mara sighed with contentment. Obviously, it wasn't her circle of friends that had needed expanding after all.

1-900-FANTASY
DANTE DAVIDSON

Ian and I found each other at a bar in Hollywood called Ye Olde Rustic Inn. It wasn't like a 1940s movie where our eyes met and held and we fell in love. It was more a floundering lunge together out of sheer necessity. Most of the other patrons were die-hard drinkers, decades older than the two of us (some older than the two of us put together).

Ian and I gravitated to each other as if pulled by a magnetic force. In the dimly lit bar, we moved from the counter to a booth in the back, and we got to know each |other over a few unhurried shots of hard liquor.

He was trying to obliterate a pretty waitress named April from his memory. I was trying to erase the fact that a handsome truck driver named Miles even existed. Together, we sat in the deep, dark vinyl booth and drank Wild Turkey and talked about the very love affairs we were doing our best to forget. We covered reasons for the breakups, and we discussed what it was about our mutual exes that we missed the most.

On that first night together, I took one of his hands in mine and turned it faceup.

"Are you a palm reader?" he asked.

"An amateur."

"What do you see in my future?"

"It's cloudy," I said, "but I can see your past. Lonely nights. Lots of them. Trying to forget—"

"Her smile," Ian would say some evenings. "Her smell," he'd say on others. "The way she looked at me when we weren't talking, you know, just sitting at some café. She'd look at me like she loved me."

"She did."

"And then I ruined it."

By having a fling with her sister, so there truly was no going back.

When it was my turn to share, I'd feel slightly less poetic than Ian. Mainly, I missed Miles's cock. And although I had been the one to officially end the relationship, it had been his mean streak that had instigated the breakup.

At some point, Ian and I realized we were talking less about our exes and more about each other. We realized we were sitting closer together in the booth, that our legs just happened to bump and our thighs rub as if our bodies had wills of their own. Weeks after our first meeting, I took his hand in mine again.

"What do you see this time?" he asked. "Still only my past?"

I shook my head. "There's a tigerish redhead in your future," I told him, and that led him to finally ask me back to his apartment at closing time. We walked the few blocks in silence, a strange occurrence for us. We were drinking buddies and talking buddies. Silence was new, startling, and difficult to deal with.

At his place, he ushered me in ahead of him and turned on the light. It was a small apartment, immaculate, with very few personal objects. He took me to the sofa and then got a bottle and two glasses. Just because we'd left the bar didn't mean we were done drinking for the night. I was happy to have a glass in my hand again. It made me feel secure.

Ian settled himself on the other end of the couch and looked at me. I could suddenly relate to the way he'd said April had looked at him. He was staring, as if mesmerized, and I had to ask, "What?" smoothing my hair, wondering if I looked worse to him out of the dim light of the bar.

"You're beautiful," he said, as if awed. "You're spectacular." I relaxed and regarded him. Ian has blond curly hair and green eyes, a strong jaw, a lopsided grin. He nudged me with his foot and I settled back into the sofa, still staring at him. We'd never had a difficult time with words, not until now, and I wondered how we were going to get over our shyness.

Ian seemed to be wondering the same thing, or focusing on the same problem, because he stood and got his cordless phone, then came back to the sofa.

"I've gotten sort of addicted to 900 numbers since the breakup," he said, something he hadn't told me before. "I've been thinking of blocking them from my phone, it's that bad."

I tilted my head at him, curious. "I've never called one before."

"They're sort of fun," he said, placing the phone at his side, reaching for my hand. I felt a charge when he began playing with my fingertips, tickling them with his. "I don't talk to the same girl, or anything. But I always get off, listening."

I felt myself growing aroused, unsure of the exact reason for the wetness in my panties. I thought for a moment, then said, "I'd like to listen while you talk on one. That is, if you wouldn't mind?"

His eyes glowed. I think he'd had the same idea. I asked next, "Do you have a separate line I could listen in on?" His studio was so small that I doubted he'd need two phones, but he surprised me by handing me the one at his side and returning with a second.

"I have one in the bedroom and one in the kitchen." He was dialing while he spoke. I lifted my receiver but he said, "I'll tell you when." Then, after a few moments, he nodded and I pressed the red button on my handset.

The woman's voice was low and husky, exactly how I would talk if I were working a sex line. I knew her goal was to keep Ian on as long as possible, and she did a good job, starting slow, asking him his name, describing herself for him, then asking his fantasy.

"Two women," he said, immediately.

"Oh," she purred. "Me and a friend of mine? Or do you have someone in mind?"

"I have someone," he said, and he moved closer to me on the sofa. He was gripping the phone with one hand, but he stroked his fingers up and down my thighs with the other.

"What's her name?"

"Miranda."

"Pretty name. Is she a pretty girl?"

"Spectacular," he said, his mouth away from the phone, his lips against my ear as he spoke.

"What do you see us doing?" she asked.

"Why don't you tell me," Ian suggested, now being more forward, cradling the phone against his shoulder and sliding both hands under my skirt. I trembled as his fingertips met my naked thighs, swallowed hard as he dragged his thumb down the sopping wet seam of my panties.

"I see us in a tub," she said, "a bubble bath. Do you like that?"

"Mmm-hmmm," Ian murmured, to keep her going.

"The three of us soaping each other all over." She was getting a little louder as she spoke, as if she were really turning herself on.

"I like that," Ian said, then looked at me and mouthed the words, "Do you like it?" and I nodded.

His fingers were probing further, up to the top of my panties and he was sliding those down my thighs and off. The woman was still talking but I could hardly concentrate on what she was saying. Ian went on his knees on the carpet, between my thighs, and he set the phone down while he moved forward to taste me. I spread my legs wide and tried to stifle the moans I so wanted to let loose.

She was still describing the scene for us. "Your girlfriend is sitting on the edge of the tub, Ian. Her pussy needs to be shaved. Do you wanna shave it or should I?"

I tapped Ian's shoulder, wanting him to pick up the

phone and talk, but he shook his head, the movement spiraling me into bliss as his whiskers tickled my outer lips. "You do it," he murmured against my skin. "You talk."

"This is Miranda," I said into the phone, startling the sex lady from her monologue. "Could you shave me? Ian's a bit busy…." The girl was good. She didn't falter. "Of course, darling. What color fur do you have down there?"

"Red," I said, sighing as Ian stroked it with his fingers, tugged gently on my curls. "Dark red."

"Pretty," she said, "But I'm gonna shave it all away and make you nice and clean for your man and me. I'm dying to taste you, and I want you bare before I give you my tongue. Would you like to be all nice and clean and pretty for me?"

I mumbled something, and she kept talking. Now I was having a hard time concentrating; between Ian and his magic tongue between my legs and this phone sex lady and her hypnotic voice I felt transported. As I neared orgasm, I handed the phone to Ian, insisted he take it from me, and he said, "Ginger? It's been a pleasure. We'll call you again."

And as he hung up the phone, I said, "Next time you'll listen while I work you." He smiled and let me know that would please him just fine.

I think we're both going to mend our broken hearts without a problem. I foresee a long and powerful love filled with sexual heat and fire in our future. I may be an amateur soothsayer, but I've got a real good feeling on this one.

In Town for Business
ZACH ADDAMS

I've always wanted to eat pussy. I have no idea if that makes me bisexual; I've always felt as gay as Julie Andrews in the Austrian Alps, but ever since I was in high school I've fantasized about having my face planted firmly between some gorgeous woman's thighs. That doesn't change the fact that most of my fantasies were about men, or that sucking cock was always my favorite thing in the world. But eating pussy came a close second—except that I'd never done it.

It's hard when you get labeled as a queer in seventh grade. You end up with lots of female best friends and you hear a lot of stories about how their boyfriends don't go down on them, but expect plenty of blow jobs. I had this one friend who was a bit of a blow job queen, with a reputation for putting out on the first date, even though she never fucked until college. She would often tell me about some new encounter where she'd had a guy's dick in her mouth and even while she was enjoying herself she had wished he would reciprocate—and as soon as she left my place I would jerk off. Imagining that I was there, eating her pussy and moving my way up to his cock just in time to have him come in both our mouths. After I'd made her come three or four times on my tongue.

When I did finally start sleeping with guys, rimming quickly became my favorite pastime. There is something so delicious about planting your tongue in a hole that's just made to receive a big cock. I always worried about those nasty parasites you can get from rimming, but that didn't stop me, it just made me meticulous about cleanliness. This annoyed me, since I loved tasting the sharp tang of boy ass, tasting every hint of his body pulsing onto my tongue as I reached between his legs and stroked his cock, listening to him moan until he came. What would it be like to just dive into a pussy and taste it in all its unwashed glory?

I wouldn't be such a dipshit as to try to explain why something turns me on, but I do remember the first piece of porn I ever found. It was a beat-up '70s sleaze paperback stuffed in my mother's nightstand drawer, and the most dog-eared of all those dog-eared pages was the one where the hero ate the heroine out for the first time, tonguing her clit over and over again until she came. The very same book had a scene where the heroine, giving some secondary male character a blow job, tucked her face between his cheeks and tongued his ass until he came. I jerked off to those two scenes more times than I can count; the moment I came I would think how weird it was that this was my mother's book, and I would be overcome with guilt as I tiptoed back to her bedroom and replaced the book after checking to make sure I hadn't gotten any of my come on it. I am quite sure that some homophobic psychoanalyst somewhere would be able to convince me that jerking off to your mother's porn will make you gay, but it's much too late to perform a controlled experiment, and how the hell would you ever get such a thing past the ethics board? My father didn't have any porn—or at least I never found it. Maybe if he had, I'd be wearing Hooters T-shirts and drinking Pabst Blue Ribbon in Fresno this very day, instead of Juicy Fruit wife-beaters and Amstel Light in the Castro.

What does it all mean? I couldn't begin to tell you, except that it means when I finally got a chance to do it, I received a round of applause that may have just turned me into the world's gayest pussyhound.

It all turned out just like one of those success stories published on an adult personals website. The original ad read: *Attractive early-thirties couple, in San Francisco this week on business, seeks very oral non-bisexual man to service both him and her. Reciprocation possible but not promised.*

Sometimes you do things and then wonder why you did them. I sent an email stating emphatically that I was not bisexual, though I suspect I was not at all what this particular couple had in mind. "Not even close to bisexual," I said, adding with a twinge of guilt at my deception, "At least, I don't think so."

I got an immediate response with a picture that made me drool. Their names were Tim and Gina. In the picture both were wearing skimpy swimsuits, his a beach thong in electric blue (tasteless) and hers a string bikini in hot pink (even more tasteless). I was not particularly interested in a fashion consultation, so I let it slide, hoping if anything happened I would be able to talk them out of their clothes quickly. He was tall and buffed, and the way his cock, half-hard in the photo, tented his tacky swimsuit made my own cock stir. But she was even more gorgeous, in that she had a body shape like Pamela Anderson's before she lost her D-cups, and bleached hair to match. She looked like the average straight guy's wet dream. That turned me on; if I was going to eat pussy for the first time, didn't it make sense to do it with a woman who could easily be in a *Hustler* spread? I imagined the woman on the cover of that early porn novel and, except for her enormous knockers, this woman looked a bit like her—if I squinted at the picture and didn't look too closely. It seemed crazy to do this, but what the hell? They probably wouldn't answer my second email, anyway.

I looked through the folder of digital photos I used when cruising guys on the Internet, and looked for the one in which I looked the least gay. There wasn't one. I finally said "fuck it" and sent a picture a friend snapped while I was working out at the gym; maybe their gaydar would be as faulty as their fashion sense.

I got an immediate response: "You free tonight?"

They were staying in an unfashionable hotel near crack row, but one that was clean enough I suspected they didn't know how many dealers were operating less than a block away. I resolved not to tell them, however tempting it might be.

As it turned out, there wasn't much of an opportunity to tell them anything.

Gina answered the door in a green terry-cloth robe that clashed so completely with her yellow hair, I immediately resolved to minimize the conversation.

"Are you Zach?" she asked.

"That's me," I told her.

"You're even cuter in person," she said. "Tim's taking a shower." I could hear water running in the bathroom.

I breathed a sigh of relief and came in to the hotel room. Gina locked the door behind me and when I took off my coat and turned around, she pushed herself up against me, grabbing my head and dragging it down to her mouth.

Never having kissed a girl before, I felt a moment's panic at the lack of beard stubble. When she opened her robe I saw that she was wearing a skimpy baby-blue-lace, see-through, one-piece thing and nothing else. I tried to think what a straight guy would do in this situation, and went right for her tits. They felt full and heavy, a little too firm—fake, maybe?—and as I tweaked her nipples the way I would tweak a guy's nipples, I heard her squeak.

"That's too hard," she said. "My nipples are very sensitive."

I felt my face reddening. Should I work harder to seem straight, or just forget it?

I decided to forget it. Not even bothering to take off my T-shirt or jeans, I pushed Gina down on the bed. I buried my face between her thighs as she spread her legs. I kissed her pussy tentatively through a thin film of baby-blue lace, smelling her cunt and feeling my cock respond immediately even as I felt the panic of bizarre newness. When she reached down and unfastened the snap crotch, I thought for a second she'd ripped it. This snap crotch thing seemed strangest of all so far.

The scent of her cunt continued to fill my nostrils, and I couldn't decide whether to be turned-on or repulsed. When I realized she was shaved smooth, I tottered into a sudden turn-on—there was something so kinky about that. Shaved balls look ridiculous in my opinion, but shaved pussies now seemed beautiful to me—even if I'd only seen them in porn. Close-up, I liked it even better.

"Eat my pussy," Gina growled.

It wasn't a request, and I didn't take it as one. I pressed my mouth to her cunt and started to lick. Her cunt tasted tangy, different from anything I'd ever experienced before. So different than a boy's butthole. But as I slipped my tongue into the tight hole, I felt a familiar lust taking me over, and I started to wriggle it deeper into her.

"Jesus," she sighed, sounding bored. "Have you ever done this before, Zach?"

Of course, I thought. *The clit. The clit. The clit.* The porn I'd read as a youngster was all about the guy jamming his enormous tongue so deep into the girl's pussy that she came uncontrollably as he tongue-fucked her. But I wasn't so gay as to be totally without clitoral knowledge. I slipped my tongue up to her clit and began to tease it, and when she responded with loud moans, I started to suck on it the way I would suck on the very tip of a guy's cock. Gina liked that.

"Shit," she moaned, sounding shocked. "Jesus, fucking Jesus!"

I kept doing that, and her fingers snaked into my hair, pushing me harder against her crotch. I had to prop one knee up on the foot of the bed to keep from sliding off, and that pushed my crotch against the edge, making me realize how hard I was. I started sucking Gina's clit in earnest, and she moaned, "Yeah, yeah, yeah, just like that, just like that, Zach, just like that," as I did. Feeling her smooth thighs and pussy against my lips, cheeks and chin made my cock throb even more. I heard the bathroom door open, but when I tried to look up, Gina's firm hand on my head kept me from moving, which only turned me on more.

Tim jumped onto the bed next to Gina and said, "Is this the guy? What's his name again?"

"Zach," she told him.

"Nice," said Tim, appraising me. I caught a glance of his gorgeous, muscled body stretched next to Gina's. He had his hard cock in his hand. He looked even bigger from this angle than he had in the photo. Tim reached down and grabbed my hair, guiding my face off of Gina's pussy and down onto his cock.

"Hey!" Gina snapped. "Don't be a pig."

"Just a little suck," said Tim. "I want to see how good he is."

I was good, from the sound of Tim's moaning as I took his cock in my mouth and began to slide up and down on him. Much as I loved his cock, though, I missed Gina's pussy, and I found myself sliding my fingers into her as she squirmed. That felt even stranger than eating her, especially since I had Tim's big cock down my throat. My cock was really throbbing now, and I knew if I just stroked it a little I would probably shoot. I swallowed Tim's cock all the way as Gina grabbed my hair.

"Gimme," she insisted, and dragged me back between her thighs. Something about having this happy suburban pervert couple fighting over me was making me even hotter. I started sucking on Gina's clit again, tonguing it rhythmically as I wrapped my hand around Tim's cock and started to stroke it. He moaned, kissing Gina and playing with her tits as I ate her out. Soon she was clamping her thighs so tightly around my face that even with my lack of experience I could tell she was going to come. God, I wanted to stroke my cock. I reached down and started to undo my pants.

"Don't come on the bedspread!" said Gina through the hoarse voice of near-orgasm.

"All right, Martha Stewart," I said, my mouth a millimeter off of her pussy. Oh, shit. That was a gay comment, wasn't it? As if to counter, I eased up my grip on Tim's cock and started eating Gina's pussy fervently.

"Jesus!" she moaned into Tim's face as she squirmed and writhed against him. He bent down and started sucking her tits as I went back to jerking his cock. When Gina came, she screamed at the top of her lungs, clawing at her husband and at the bedspread I wasn't supposed to come on. I had to stop stroking my cock to keep from doing exactly that.

When Gina finally pushed my face away from her pussy, shuddering with the remnants of her orgasm, she seemed more ravenous than ever. She dragged me onto the bed and yanked off my shirt, then pulled my jeans all the way open and began to suck my cock as Tim pushed his mouth to mine.

Again, I felt the curious lack of stubble as her face bobbed up and down on my shaft. But even stranger was the feeling of Tim kissing me—totally unexpected, since I'd figured he was straight, or thought he was. His hand curved around the base of my cock and fed it to Gina as we kissed. Then he got up on his knees and crouched over me, holding my head to guide his cock into my mouth.

In this position I couldn't do the thrilling job of cocksucking I was used to, but I managed just fine. Putting my hands up to play with Tim's nipples, I sucked on the head of his cock and, when I heard him moaning like he was going to come, reached down again to stroke the base of his shaft. Feeling Gina's mouth glide up and down on my shaft made me want all of Tim's come more than I'd ever wanted anything. He clutched the headboard, swearing at the top of his lungs as he shot his load into my mouth and I eagerly gulped. When he finished coming, he slid off of me in an instant and, to my surprise, I felt his mouth joining Gina's on my cock.

They traded off sucking me, and the sight of both of them opening wide for my shaft turned me on more than anything. Especially since I'd fully expected to leave without even getting a cursory hand job. I was moaning so loud and thrashing back and forth so wildly that I couldn't even begin to tell you who finally got my load in their mouth, but I could definitely feel the clamp of someone's firm lips halfway down my shaft, his or her tongue eagerly working the underside to milk my come. I couldn't tell you definitely which one of them swallowed my come, but I like to think it was Tim.

There was no cuddling afterward, no "you give great head," just a quick, "Thanks," from Gina and a nervous, "You know we never do that," from Tim.

"Me either," I told them, and dabbed my spit-covered cock and pussy-slick face with the same white hotel towel.

So what does it all mean? Bisexual is such a strange word, and however much I love pussy I still feel gayer than Liza Minnelli in a leotard and fishnets.

I still love sex with guys more than anything. But you'd be amazed at how easy it is to pick up chicks in San Francisco when all you can think of doing is eating their pussies and sucking their boyfriends' cocks. Maybe they know that I've got a lot of time to make up for. Very few of them look like Pamela Anderson, but then, very few of them insist that I not be bisexual. So I don't bother telling them one way or another, and if anyone asks, I'm the world's gayest pussyhound. Call *Guinness* if you want. Or, better yet, just call my cell phone.

If You Can Make It There, You Can Make It Anywhere

A. J. STONE

For Wyatt

It's an early fall night when the weather hovers between thoughts of summer, hot and sticky, and then changes its mind and whips into the frenzy of fall. My skin reacts, stands away from bone, supported by fine hairs, and my nipples grow hard, as if touched by a finger or a tongue. It's late. A girls' night out—my friend Nathalie and I have splurged on a new and fashionable restaurant downtown just above Wall Street, a neighborhood as sly and mysterious as the weather. Nathalie and I have known each other for years. We roomed together briefly when Nathalie first came to New York; now she lives uptown in an apartment which, until recently, she shared with Mark, her boyfriend of five years. The restaurant is thick with businessmen on expense accounts, pungent with testosterone, cocks at attention and ready to pounce. Nathalie and I gossip and drink round balloons of red wine that pop down our throats and make us as giggly as if we had sniffed helium. Two women in a room full of men, the first women most of them have seen all day apart from their dowdy secretaries or their female colleagues. Two women dressed in revealing clothing—low-cut dresses that slip and tease. A glimpse of nipple, a thigh unconsciously rubbed. Dresses of thin silk that slips into the cracks of our asses as we walk. Dresses clearly worn over no underwear. Dresses to frustrate. A few men buy us drinks but we're not biting. I have another goal in mind: the blonde sitting across the table from me. Curiosity has been an unspoken dance between us for years, frustrated by our other obligations. Suddenly, we are single at the same time.

We skirt around the tension between us, pumping it up by discussing sex, the first time, the best time, the craziest time. Nathalie puts down her fork in the middle of the main course—medallions of black cod—and runs a hand through her blonde hair. There is a moment of silence before she speaks.

"Remember the week Mark was away on business and we went out to that sushi place and got drunk on sake?" she begins.

I remember that, and passing out on Nathalie's bed.

"When I woke up, sometime around dawn, I had a terrible headache. I downed a couple of aspirin but I threw them right up. There was this…well…trick I'd learned in college. You were sound asleep…," Nathalie falters, embarrassed, the color rising in her cheeks.

"Go on," I urge her, one hand beneath my napkin, playing with my dress.

Nathalie plunges onward. She had pulled up her nightgown and masturbated while I slept soundly beside her.

"I was so afraid you'd wake up," she says and looks at me, then adds nervously, "I have to use the ladies' room."

When she is gone, I signal for the check. I'm not wearing any underwear and I can feel a trail of liquid snaking down my thigh. Nathalie catches my eye as she makes her way across the room but I can't tell if her eyes are large with fear or desire. The eyes of the other diners follow us as we leave, their cocks thick and swollen. I can bet there'll be a lot of pounced-on wives tonight, visions of Nathalie and me beckoning forward more than one orgasm. The streets are dark and deserted and shadowed. I weave down the street, dancing to too many glasses of wine echoing in my head, my dark hair as wild as a tussle beneath the sheets. A tune goes off in Nathalie's head. She spins me and the world with me and I am thrown against a wall. A brief moment and then her tongue is in my mouth, tentative, slight, a drunken experiment, and when she backs away, amazed at her boldness, she leaves me hungry, my nipples reaching out. We walk down the street laughing and I tease her about it.

"Do you want to feel my wet pussy?" I ask her, looking at her out of the corner of my eye, challenging her. She's unable to answer but I can feel the lump in her throat. She's never done this before and frankly, neither have I, but the wine, the attention of the men in the restaurant, and her confession have made me horny and curious. I need to be touched, even if I do it myself. And, exhibitionist that I am, I want to be *watched.*

I lift my dress. Underneath I am wearing stay-up stockings. I circle my clit with my finger, beckoning her forward. First with my eyes and then, "Nathalie," I beg, my throat as thick and swollen as my cunt. She touches me tentatively, her fingers brushing my hard clit. I moan and close my eyes, then will them open. I want to see her desire, her curiosity, as she sinks her fingers into me. Does she know that I've been wet all evening, willing her to do this? Does she know how many times my finger circled my clit at dinner, my eyes creamy not from candlelight but the look down the long slide toward orgasm? Her face is closed to my scrutiny.

I want her to sink her face into my pussy and I tell her so. But she is hesitant. She has not yet found the audacity of desire. I won't push her yet, although I'm eager to have her mouth on my clit, her tongue deep inside me. I can feel an orgasm barreling down my body. I want to hear my screams echo off the canyons made by the buildings. I want windows wide open and neighbors' heads thrust out, an audience to my cries. I reach out to touch her and she backs away, but not before I have cupped my hand between her legs. Her cunt beneath her dress is swollen and ripe. She is as wet as I am and I wonder if she stroked herself in the bathroom, bringing herself just to the brink of orgasm. Nervous, she wiggles her hips from my slender hand, but not before I have pushed the front of her dress, light armor that only barely shields her naked cunt from my hand, into her. Her juices leave an imprint on the thin fabric.

I suggest a cab but they are difficult to find at this time of night and we begin to walk. She sucks on her fingers, tasting me for the first time, and I play with my nipple, hard through my dress as she watches me, unable to look away. I tell her I want her tongue on me, rough and strong. I can see that her defenses are beginning to drop and beneath her dress, her nipples are as tight as mine. At the corner, a taxi with its off-duty sign slows down for a red light and I step down from the curb.

I roll my window down reluctantly. Instantly I know these two girls are drunk; their eyes are too bright. But I'm going uptown anyway and I figure I might as well make a decent fare off it. They scramble into the back and give me two addresses.

It's late and I'm tired and I'm gunning for home and a few clicks across the porn channels before I pass out, my spent cock in my hand. The thought is enticing and I drive fast. It's strangely quiet in the backseat. And then I catch moaning. Damn, I think, two drunk girls. That's all I need, one of them sick in the backseat and an extra half hour while I have to clean it out, not to mention a little something less in my paycheck when they've got to take the whole car in for a shampoo. I glance up at the rearview mirror to check the backseat. The dark-haired girl, in a thin dress, coat off her shoulders, lies against one window, eyes half-mast, her hand lazily circling her nipple. The moans are coming from her mouth. I slow down, my cock suddenly hard and pulsing, straining to catch a glimpse of the other girl. I find her blonde head bobbing up and down, buried between the legs of the dark-haired one. I can't really see what's going on but I begin to guess, my imagination racing, as the dark-haired girl's moans direct her friend's movements. I raise my eyes and we catch each other in the mirror for a brief moment before she turns away. She must know I'm watching, listening, because she keeps looking up, her eyes seeking mine. I strain to catch her words as she begins narrating, her voice thick with lust. *Lick me, suck my clit,* she says. She pulls her dress down a little further and her nipple, pink and taut, springs free. *Oh,* a little sigh escapes from my mouth. I want my mouth on that nipple, to circle it with my tongue and bite on it and feel her clit jump against my swollen cock. *Oh, yes,* she moans, and every promise leaps out from her eyes. I'm imagining her, slick and tight, riding my cock. The cab slows as I stroke myself, pumping my cock in my fist, trying to keep my mind on driving. A red light up ahead brings my eyes back to the road. The light is green too quickly and I wish for another excuse to stop so I can use my other hand to pull at my balls, stretching the skin tightly over my cock. I search the rearview mirror for the black eyes of the dark-haired girl.

The cabdriver agrees to take us both uptown with a first stop at my house and then on to Nathalie's and we scramble into the back. I have a goal that doesn't involve a second stop but I don't argue when Nathalie pipes in with her address. I get in first and Nathalie hangs back for a moment, as shy and eager as the new girl in school who dreams of being a cheerleader, before she scoots in beside me. Then she slams the door and by the time she has settled herself beside me I've pulled my skirt up and have begun playing with myself in earnest, my head leaning against the window, one hand manipulating my clit, the other hand pulling my nipples into hard points. For a moment, Nathalie can only watch in fascination, her mouth open. And then I see her tongue, moving quickly back and forth against her front teeth, debating. I push back the lips of my pussy, my clit swollen and red between them, as an offering.

"Please…," my voice begs.

I want her kneeling between my legs, sucking at my clit—I want her so badly that I almost begin to weep. I know that I could bring myself to orgasm quickly. I also know how unsatisfying that would be.

"What do I…," Nathalie's voice falters, confused, worried about what to do in this unfamiliar, familiar territory.

I plunge my fingers into my cunt, hitting my G-spot, and for a moment there is nothing but my cunt, my fingers. I will myself reluctantly back to the present, back to the goal. My fingers are luminescent with my own juice and I reach over, slipping them into Nathalie. Her hips press into my hand. She looks at me, then down at my fingers moving in and out of her cunt and then back at me and I can see the astonishment on her face. Nothing in her experience has prepared her for this—not Mark, three nights a week, not Joe, the best-sex-ever, not even Ian, the one-night stand who introduced her to anal sex. Her hips move in circles and her clit retreats and I can feel, from the way her muscles tighten, how fast her orgasm is building. But I don't want her to come just yet. That will be later, when I have time to explore her, tease her, stretched out on my bed. Right now I want to pull her to the edge of desire, the place where all of her inhibitions disappear and there is nothing but body and want and need and hunger. She grabs my retreating hand and forces my fingers to her mouth, sucking each one slowly, telling me in silent language how much she wants me. I moan, pulsing in time to the motion of her mouth. With her other hand she begins to explore me, first tentatively, then more insistently, her fingers parting my pubic hair, pulling at the curls. Her head bends forward to examine me and I can feel her hot breath and I rise to meet her mouth. I groan, my eyes rising, and briefly meet the eyes of the cabdriver in the rearview mirror. His eyes are large and dark and I recognize the look in them and know that his cock is hard in his fist. Another moan escapes my lips. Nathalie's tongue darts out, hard and pointy, and laps at my cunt, following my fingers' lead, my pleas. My moans give her courage and she rakes at my clit with her teeth, pulling the lips down, her tongue exploring the crevices, my clit in her mouth being sucked like a small cock. She teases me, stopping and starting, knowing the rhythms of my cunt as she knows her own. I break the gaze of the cabdriver and watch Nathalie's movements intently as she inserts two fingers into me and I begin the slide into orgasm. I have only come like this a few times in my life, hovering between life and death, and when the explosions have ended, I pull Nathalie's head up and kiss her on the lips, tasting myself on her. When the cab jerks suddenly, I know that our driver has not been far behind....

I try to keep focused on the road, periodically glancing into the backseat where the dark-haired girl has locked her gaze on mine. My hand moves with her friend's head bobbing up and down and I know how warm and wet that blonde's mouth would be, wrapped around my cock. The dark-haired girl looks away and I'm frantic, trying to catch her eye. My rhythm falters for a moment. But the growing series of moans from the backseat is a command my cock cannot resist. My hips buck upward, my foot jerking on the gas pedal and I empty myself into my hand, the dark-haired girl's screams a call that pulls my orgasm from me in violent spasms as I turn the corner to the first stop....

"Just below the streetlamp," I tell the driver, "then you can take her…"

Nathalie interrupts me before I have a chance to finish. "No second stop," she says.

I look over at her as she springs out of the cab, already halfway up the steps to my apartment, and then I lean forward to check the fare. The driver and I study each other's faces in the light, my mouth slick with my own juice, and then he catches my eye and an understanding passes between us. I reach into my wallet and press a bill into his hand. He closes my fingers around the crisp currency.

"My pleasure," he says.

The wine whispers the Sinatra lyric to me as I scramble up the steps. *If I can make it there, I'll make it anywhere.* Nathalie pulls me to her, reaching over to suck on my earlobe. Then the door to my apartment clicks open and we are inside.

Trepidation

RACHEL KRAMER BUSSEL

Tonight is going to be the sexiest night of my life, by far—if I can get past my nerves enough to appreciate my dream come true: a threesome with the hottest guy and girl I've ever met. I asked for this. I instigated it all by myself. Still, I'm nervous. It's my naughty dream, the one I jerk off to late at night all alone. I never actually thought it would happen, and I'm beginning to wonder if I should've kept it in fantasyland. But now there's no going back.

It started as a daydream; I was lying in bed, and when my hands started to drift towards my cunt, all I could think of was me, naked, eyes shut, with the two people who most turn me on (and terrify me) beating and stroking and caressing and spanking me. The more I thought about it, the more turned-on I got. After a few weeks of this scene popping up unbidden to play in my mind at all hours of the day and night, it wasn't just my number one fantasy, it was my only fantasy.

I was hesitant to tell my lover, Kevin. Would he go there with me? We talk all the time, and I've told him I'd love to do the most wicked of things, like have him blindfold me and take me somewhere public, someplace I might run into people I know, and fuck me senseless. We've talked about plenty of filthy fantasy scenarios that make me come like a rocket, ones I'd never contemplate actually trying in real life.

But this was different; this one touched me to my core, made me willing to sacrifice any last shred of remaining dignity, suffer any potentially embarrassing discomfort, even risk my most treasured relationships for one night of the most incredible sex I could imagine. Just the idea of it sent chills throughout my body, ones that seemed to keep me permanently aroused no matter how many times I came.

That persistence is what pushed me to finally tell Kevin. I mentioned it casually one day, hoping he couldn't hear my heart pounding away, and things took off from there.

Despite how long we've been dating or how close we've gotten, Kevin remains an enigma to me, a powerful, strong top who can pin me down in seconds, but also a shy, sensitive soul who cries more often than I do. I love him dearly and know him as well as anyone can, which, sadly for me, is only so far, never as much as I crave. I'm aware of demons that lurk in the dark caves of his mind where I can never quite seem to reach. I know that sometimes an innocent comment, a flirty suggestion, will trigger a reaction far removed from the one I'd wanted. His moodiness wreaks havoc on us, and I have to feel him out on even the smallest decisions or risk losing him to his private world.

It's not that he's fickle or mean or uncaring, but there are parts of his past he holds so close I doubt any lover's ever learned of them. So I thought he might be more likely to go for wild public sex than this most intimate private act I was proposing. Little did I know that his fantasies veered along the same course as mine, though he'd never mentioned this little fact to me in all our wild naked tale-spinning. Turns out he had a little crush on Betty too, had pictured her naked, pictured me with her countless times. He hadn't ever let on, even though he was the one who introduced me to her and he had seen my eyes widen as I took in her sexy shoes, her tall, imposing, curvaceous body. But that was Kevin, always making me work to get at his thoughts, even if that meant he cut off his nose to spite his dick. Now that the truth was out, our path was set.

So I waited patiently, as ordered, while they got together to seal my fate. The woman in my fantasies wasn't just any woman, not some simpering bisexual stereotype who would walk in and fulfill some stereotypical fantasy of curves and soft skin and delicately-placed kisses. No, I didn't want some generic woman to complement my most individual of men, but her, Betty, the beautiful, outrageous Amazon we were both desperately attracted to.

They asked me if I wanted to know in advance what would happen, and I demurred. That would ruin it for me. Of course a part of me was dying of curiosity, but the real rebel in me, the one who gets off on being taken to new and unfamiliar sexual territory, who wanted to be brought to tears and scared out of her wits, wanted to know as little as possible of what awaited me.

Finally the appointed evening arrives. They take me to dinner at an Italian restaurant of their choosing. I pick at my food and barely even make conversation, but when I am deemed too sullen or distant Kevin sharply taps my hand, or Betty yanks my hair. I'm so aroused I almost have to reach under the table to make sure I'm not gushing all over at the sight of them sneaking conspiratorial looks at each other across the table. I wait as long as possible, but when I finally rush to the bathroom to check myself I'm sure that all the other women crowding the vanity can smell just how very wet I am. Back at the table, every look from either of them, every double-edged comment, every bite of food they take heightens my anticipation, yet I don't know exactly what I'm anticipating. It's so deliciously maddening I want to scream, but I grind my teeth instead.

After what feels like an eternity, we exit the restaurant. All this time they've been carrying on a seemingly normal conversation about work and politics, occasionally referring to me in the third person, as if this was one more of their planning sessions, while I sat patiently, silent for the most part, my head filled with infinite visions of glorious debauchery. I like the way they've been talking about me, like I'm theirs to do with as they please, because it's true, I most definitely am. There aren't too many people you can safely invite to treat you like a piece of meat. Tonight, I forget about anything outside of our special threesome, our perfectly-in-sync trio of lust, and give myself over to them.

We get out of the car and they steer me into the house, coddling me, their hands warm and gentle, for now. We go upstairs and they slowly, worshipfully, remove each piece of my clothing, unrolling my stockings down to my toes, then lifting them off and placing them carefully on a chair. There's none of the usual clothes ripping and flying across the room tonight. None of the frenzied madness that usually ensues with Kevin, when we are much too horny and impatient to make it to the bed and find ourselves pressed against each other in the hallway or on the stairs. Tonight, Kevin and Betty both act as if they haven't a care in the world, ignoring my state of heightened horniness while their hands move slowly and patiently. Each soft touch makes me want to force them to unleash their full erotic energy. Are they simply buttering me up before taking me down?

I'm left in only my black silk panties, which by now are completely soaked with my juices, as I'm made to sit in a wooden chair like a naughty schoolgirl sent in to see both the principal *and* vice principal. I look down at my lap, unable to face either of them, while Kevin taunts me. "You've been a very naughty girl, haven't you? Trying to orchestrate this little evening, letting us know just how much pain you want, what torturous treats you wish to be subjected to. I guess I'm not good enough for you—you didn't have a good time last night when I made you come nine times? You always want more and more and more, don't you? I know the way you look at Betty, the way you think of her putting her hands all over you. I knew long before you told me about this fantasy of yours. Tell me what you want, you little brat," he snarls at me as he pulls my hair, harder than he ever has before. I can feel my scalp tightening, the skin on my forehead inching up, and with each pull I feel a corresponding tightening in my pussy.

I shift without consciously thinking about it. He notices

and lets go of my hair, fast, then puts his hand on the back of my head, pulls me from the chair, and shoves me onto the bed, facedown, splayed out across the mattress. In a second, he pulls down my panties, spreads my bare legs and plunges his fingers inside my cunt, knowing I'll be wet for him. This feels good and safe. He is testing me, making sure I'm ready for him. I am breathing so heavily I'm sure they can both hear how much I want them. I squirm and try to pull his fingers deeper into me but he takes them out. He walks around me in a half-circle, trying to decide the exact position he wants me in. I can hear Betty moving around the room but I don't look up, suddenly shy and embarrassed at what I've gotten myself into.

My whole body is trembling. I'm on the verge of calling this off, and I start to feel like I do at parties where I don't know anyone, where I want to hide in the bathroom until it's all over or in a bedroom curled up in a blanket with a cup of tea. There's no tea or blankets in sight, only the feel of my legs spread as wide apart as they can be, of the underused muscles in my thighs straining against the sensation, flexing and arching, raring to go. But go where? I can't tell where I want to go, and I realize this is part of the reason I've asked to be here, so I don't have to know where to go; someone else will decide that for me.

All these thoughts are racing through my head when suddenly I feel the cold lube sliding along the crack of my asshole. I feel her fingers, soft and smooth, coating it on, pouring more, rubbing it up and around and all over. My asshole clenches, blocking the lube's entry, and then opens, letting some of it in as she teases me, her finger gently pressing against my hole but not entering. I hear fumbling and some muted whispers, and then her finger enters my ass and I twitch crazily, thrashing all around as she slowly presses into my most sensitive area. I am dying for him to put his fingers, or his cock, back in my pussy; for something, anything to fill this cloying hole inside me, this insurmountable need, but I simply shut my eyes tight and bite my arm, afraid to jinx things. They know what is best for me.

I try to let go and calm my mind but I can't. The more I try not to think about her finger slowly pushing its way into my asshole, the more that is the only thing I can think about. I try squeezing my pussy and feel myself tighten around her finger. "You want more, don't you, you little minx? I know all about what you like. Kevin filled me in, he told me exactly what kind of a filthy whore you are." I jerk when she says the magic word—*whore*—the word that Kevin knows will always make me spread my legs wider, will always instill in me the urge to be fucked harder. "That's right, you're our whore tonight, and we don't even have to pay you. You're going to let us have our way with you for free, let us do anything we want no matter how filthy it is. I'm gonna leave marks all over you to make sure that everyone who sees you knows that I fucked you good and hard, so that when you take a shower or look in the mirror you'll remember every minute of tonight." She is speaking in a harsh whisper and her words send waves of heat coursing through me.

She stops talking and for a moment there is dead silence in the room, and then she does what I've been dreaming about—she pulls her finger from my ass and begins to spank me. She doesn't warm me up first like Kevin does, with light taps that prepare my body for what's to come; no, she starts full force, slapping me hard as can be on one cheek and then the other, alternating but going so fast that I simply feel a continuous assault of pain. She scrapes her bright red nails down my ass, digging them in briefly before resuming her treatment. I can feel each smack reverberate through my pussy, feel my juices slowly dripping down my thighs. Just as I am starting to shake, quivering and on the verge of coming, she stops. "I think it's time," she says to Kevin, and I bury my head in the pillow, knowing there will be no turning back.

Kevin leans over me and fumbles with something that I quickly realize is a blindfold, and I happily oblige as he straps it around my head. I want to feel everything, focus on each sensation they unleash upon me, and the lack of sight will help sharpen all my other senses. I can hear them each making appraising comments—"Good ass," "She looks quite sturdy"— simple statements meant to put me in my place as their toy, their object, their plaything. And it works; I am no longer me, Janice, a whole person with an outside, professional, interesting life; I am only what I can offer to them, from the top of my head to the bottoms of my feet.

Now fingers are probing my slit, stroking along my opening until I feel like I will die if they don't enter me. They stop, and I spread my legs as wide as I can, urging them onward. I feel two sets of hands roving up and down my body, stroking, pinching, teasing as they lightly trail along my skin and send shivers wherever they go. I have ceased trying to figure out who is doing what, and just when I've all but given up on getting fucked the way I most want to, I feel something enter me, stretching my cunt until I cry out in pleasure. It must be the biggest dildo ever, sliding inside me inch by slow inch. But they are not done: I feel another invasion, something sliding along the tender skin of my asshole, pushing and probing, and I relax and let it in. Now I am completely filled and they both croon to me, telling me what a good girl I am to take so much, so fast, as each toy is worked in and out in tandem. I let out a sound that is half moan, half garbled sob, and relax into the sensation of being plundered beyond belief. They are working extra hard to push me past my limits, beyond the realm of anything I've experienced before, testing my body, and all I know is that I want to pass this test, want to make both of them proud of me. I am their little girl, their toy, their student—whatever they want me to be.

They turn me over, and the butt plug presses against me in the most agonizing way, and as I squirm they each pin down an arm, and Betty leans forward and kisses me, her perfect lips soft and hot and juicy. The kiss is an oasis of tenderness, a heavenly caress in the midst of their plundering. Then their slow assault suddenly picks up its pace and they are fucking me again hard and fast. Betty is slamming the dildo into me with one hand while pressing on my neck with the other, allowing just enough air for me to breathe and just enough pressure to send even more heat throughout my body. Kevin presses his thumb hard against my clit, just the right motion to send me orbiting, orgasm crashing down all around me as my ass and pussy clench madly.

But still we are not done, far from it. They slide the toys out of me, and somehow, instead of being tired or sore, I simply want more. Instead of keeping the blindfold on, they make me watch. Kevin spreads me out on my back and teases me with his cock, sliding it just inside, then out again. After a few minutes he gets up and Betty takes over, her lubed-up fingers slipping and sliding into my cunt, twisting and turning, pushing and pressing until I feel like I will explode. My mouth is open, moaning and sighing, and Kevin slides his cock between my lips, hovering over me, his trembling cock a most delicious sight. I have to focus on taking him into me, on making sure my neck is at the right angle, and I do, sucking and pulling him further inside as Betty pushes even deeper, sliding her thumb in to join her other fingers, pressing her whole hand into me, filling me up more than any toy ever could. Now I am totally theirs, my body fully invaded, taken over in the most glorious of ways. I writhe and twist, squeeze and suck, but never struggle. I close my eyes and shiver as I give myself—my mouth, my cunt, my being—to them. Kevin can't resist the way I suck his cock for long, eagerly tightening my cheeks, stroking my tongue along the underside of his shaft, and he pulls out, splashing my neck and chest with his warm come. At the sight of his jizz spurting out, his face contorted in agony, I come a second time, clenching Betty's hand for all I'm worth. I look at my gorgeous pair of lovers, old and new, both all mine, at least for tonight, and smile the smile of the truly sated, of the gloriously fucked, of one whose fantasy has not just been fulfilled, but enhanced and perfected beyond belief. They have given me what I wanted all along, and gazing at them, I see that I'm exactly where I'm supposed to be.

Cast of Three

EMILIE PARIS

My husband and I work at home. Jonathan is a webmaster and I'm a freelance writer. Some of our friends tease us, winking as they wonder aloud if we lounge all day in silk pajamas and satin robes. If they only knew….

On a recent Friday morning, while I was speaking on the phone with one of my editors, Jonathan came into my office. His faded khakis were open at the fly, and his unbuttoned denim work shirt revealed his broad chest, muscular from many hours of nightly workouts. I met his gaze and instantly understood the yearning, hungry look in his eyes. As I continued talking to Fiona, I watched Jonathan take out his cock and begin stroking it slowly, deliberately.

My editor, oblivious on the other end of the line, spoke to me of dashes and commas, of new paragraphs and run-on sentences. All the while, Jon's hand worked faster on his cock, the ridge of his palm slamming against his body as skin moved on skin. That clapping sound was undeniably erotic, and I could feel a rush of heat color my cheeks. I love watching my husband jerk off. His brow furrows. His sea-green eyes squeeze shut. Near the end, his head goes back, revealing the seductive line of his long neck. I can see him swallow hard, steel himself as he tries not to let loose. Then, as he approaches his peak, he talks. Murmurs, really. Nonsense words, or unfinished words. Sometimes he says my name, whispers it.

Fiona was saying it now. "*Gina,* are you listening?"

"I'm fine," I said. "I mean, I'm here. Could I—?" I was starting to say, "Could I call you back?" but Jonathan stopped me, shaking his head quickly as he took a step in my direction. He didn't want me to get off the phone.

"Could you repeat that last bit?" I asked, shooting him a questioning glance.

He answered with actions rather than words. Moving closer, he placed the head of his throbbing cock against my glossed lips, butting forward. I sucked him easily, the phone still cradled in my hand, his cockhead cradled between my parted lips. The tip of my pink tongue flicked out, up and down his shaft. While I worked him, I tried not to make any noise, moved away from him when I had to give a response to Fiona.

With my focus shifted from Fiona to fucking, I could no longer comprehend what my editor was saying, but I was still able to make those *mm-hmmm* comfort sounds that tend to appease her. She continued speaking to me about a recent project, one that she'd liked but that needed minor changes. Changes like the shift and pull of Jon's cock in my mouth, minor edits like the way he dragged the head of his cock along the roof of my mouth, reveling in the ridged texture against his smooth skin.

Finally, Fiona said, "That's about it, Gina. Call me when you have a fresh draft."

"Mm-hmmm," I said again, pulling back from Jon and adding a "good-bye" before hanging up the phone. I thought my husband would ravish me then and there. I was sure he'd turn me around in the leather office chair, lower my well-worn jeans, place the slick, wet head of his cock between my slender thighs, and enter my dripping pussy. A good, satisfying fuck is one of my all-time favorite ways to start the day. But Jon had other ideas. Leaning across my desk, he asked, "What's Victoria's number?"

"Why?" I asked. Already, I had one hand between my legs, cupping my cunt through the crotch of my jeans, rocking on the seam that pressed perfectly against my clit. I could already sense how good this climax was going to be.

"Just tell me."

His cock pointed forward, like a divining rod. I blinked, thought of my ex-roommate's number, and rattled it off from memory before realizing what he was doing. Yet, somewhere in my head, I knew. Of course I knew. This was one of Jonathan's four-star fantasies in motion. And all I had to do was play along.

While I watched, he dialed the number quickly and then handed me the phone. "Victoria Morris, please," I said when the receptionist answered. As I talked my way through Vicky's personal assistant, Jon moved me around, so that my ass was toward him. Swiftly, he lowered my jeans down my thighs, leaving them on but out of his way.

"I liked the way you handled Fiona," he said, as I waited for Vicky to answer the phone. "See if you can keep it up."

Vicky is a high-level attorney, but I knew she wouldn't mind a call at work. Still, I couldn't immediately think of anything to say as Jon's cock worked its powerful way into my tight cunt. He had one hand around my waist, and his fingers lingered lightly between the lips of my pussy. Luckily, when Vicky came on the line, I had a sudden brain wave.

"Hey, Vick," I said. "I was wondering if we could have lunch together Friday."

"Let me check my schedule." I could hear the beeping from her electronic date book. As she scrolled through the week, she said, "How's life at home? You guys getting any work done, or are you just fucking around?"

"I'm getting a lot taken care of," I said, grinning, feeling those wondrous inner muscles of my pussy begin to helplessly contract on the head of Jon's cock. At this move, his breathing grew more ragged. I looked into the window above my desk and could see a ghostly reflection of the two of us. My long, auburn hair was pulled back in a no-nonsense ponytail, and as I watched, Jon pulled the ribbon free, letting my curls fall loose around my shoulders. He gripped into my hair with one hand, pulling my head back hard. Feeling the power behind that move, I wondered how long I'd be able to keep up a normal-sounding conversation.

Vicky had found Friday at last. "I've got a mid-morning meeting that might go late. How's one o'clock?"

"One's great," I managed to answer. "I'll meet you in the lobby."

"Got another call, Gina. Be good," she said, and she was gone.

Be *good?* As good as I could possibly be, as good as anyone could be in that situation. I was rocked with the motions of Jon's body against mine. His cock slammed forward and then withdrew, leaving just the mushroom head inside me. The scent of my arousal was light in the air. Jonathan always says my pussy smells like perfume, like flower petals, but I don't agree. I think I have a richer scent—slightly spicy—just before I come. And right now, I was about to come. Jon sensed it. Grabbing my waist, he pulled me back against him. My office chair is on wheels, and the whole piece of furniture moved with me, rocking us both. Jon seemed to like that, and he gripped the arms of the chair and fucked me using the motion of the wheels. Then, his breathing harsh, he said, "Call Sarah."

"Come on, Jon." I was dying, caught in the moment of not wanting to come because it felt so good but almost coming anyway because I couldn't fucking help it. If he would just keep up the rhythm, I'd climax in no time.

"Call her, Gina."

"Please," I said. "I'm almost there."

"Just call her up."

Jon knew I was stalling for time, just playing with him. He brought his hand down on my rear, giving me a playful love-spank to make me obey. I hesitated for one more moment, winning myself another spank before caving in to his desires. My ass smarted from the open-handed smack, and I reached back to rub the sore spot before lifting the phone.

Sarah's our next-door neighbor. I have her number on our speed dial and, staring into Jon's reflection, I picked up the handset and pressed one button. She's an artist and works at home, too. I could hear her phone ringing through the connecting wall of our townhouses.

"Talk dirty this time," Jon said, grabbing my asscheeks with both hands, pawing me hard enough to leave marks.

"Dirty?"

"You know, baby."

He was right. I knew. As I said, this was Jon's favorite fantasy in motion, an X-rated sex play with a cast of three. Who was I to knock it off course? I held the phone to my ear and waited, impatiently, for Sarah to answer. She picked up on the fifth ring.

"Hey, it's Gina," I managed to squeak out as Jon pulled his cock, wet and sticky, from my cunt and began making thrusting moves with the head between the cheeks of my ass. I trembled, knowing exactly what he was going to do and wondering how I was going to talk through it.

"What's up, girl?"

My heart rate, I thought. "Nothing," I said, "just procrastinating."

"Still in your pajamas?"

Jon moved back and forth, rubbing the length of his rock-hard cock along the split of my ass before oiling it up with his spit and thrusting the first inch inside me. I would have moaned aloud if I hadn't been talking to Sarah. Instead, I said, "PJs? You think I wear pajamas?"

"You're right, Gina," she said apologetically. "You're much more of a T-shirt and panties kind of girl."

"How about you?" I asked, envisioning her thick black hair falling over her shoulders, her slender body draped in something long and sheer and silky. "What are *you* wearing?"

"Nothing," Sarah said, and her voice sounded as raw as Jon's. I could tell that my kinky husband liked the way this conversation was going, because he suddenly slipped in another inch of his bone. I bit my lip to stifle the sound of a moan as he whispered, "Invite her over."

"How can you paint when you're not wearing anything?" I asked, my voice trembling. Jon had stopped moving, his cock now tucked deep in my ass, his hands resting lightly on my waist. I squeezed him rhythmically with my muscles, but still managed to reach forward and press the speaker button on our phone.

"I'm not painting, silly," Sarah said to the captive audience of two. "I'm listening to you guys do it."

"How'd you know...?" I asked, as Jon started moving again inside me.

"The squeak of your wheels against the wood floor. It's got a very familiar sound to it. And he's making you call people again, isn't he?"

"Get over here, kid," Jon said, continuing his throbbing pace in my ass, grabbing the arms of the chair again and letting Sarah hear the squeak of the wheels.

"On my way."

Jon leaned over me to hang up the phone, pressing his cock all the way to the hilt as he did. I sighed and then moaned aloud, no longer playing the role of the hardworking freelancer.

Sarah has a key to our apartment. For emergencies. Or times when we're out of town and she brings in the mail. Or mornings when the three of us decide that what we really need to get done is not our work but each other. The door opened only moments later, and we heard her padding in bare feet down the hall. Quickly, I turned to see my best friend standing in the doorway.

"Now isn't this a pretty picture," she said, smiling. "I should have brought my easel."

Jon motioned for her to join us.

"Where do you want me, Jonny?" Sarah asked. "On the table so I can kiss your pretty wife, or on my knees behind you so I can lick your asshole until you shoot?"

Sarah can talk like a trucker. It's one of her best features, and it was obvious from his expression that Jon didn't know what he wanted. Both scenarios were equally arousing. But after brief consideration, he took a breath and said, "Start with Gina. She needs you."

Did I ever. I needed her perched on my polished wood desk so that I could run my hands up and down her supple body. Needed her pouting lips parted against my own so that I could meet her tongue with mine. She had slipped on a robe, and I nearly tore it in my haste to see her naked. As soon as I did, I realized that she hadn't lied to me. She'd been listening to us fuck, and the sounds had turned her on. I could tell from the way her shaved pussy lips were already glistening with her personal lubrication.

"I want to taste you," I said.

Sarah didn't seem to have a problem with this idea. But she did have a problem with the location. There was no comfortable place for her to sit. Jon took care of the situation swiftly, picking me up while still inside of me and moving me onto the floor. Sarah took up her position in front of me immediately, parting her toned thighs and then staring to see if I would follow through with my offer. I could hardly wait. With Jon slipping back and forth in my ass, I bent and brought my tongue to Sarah's carefully shaved cunt, French-kissing her throbbing clit and making her moan loudly. Luckily, we're the only freelancers in our line of townhouses. There was nobody else to be disturbed by the sounds of us getting together.

"Lick her clit," Jon told me, in his directing mode. "Make her come hard."

That was my plan, exactly. Taking over from where her fingers had obviously left off, I got her up to our speed in no time. My tongue made tricks and spirals and figure eights around her hot little button. I slid it into her hole and pressed in deep, tongue-fucking her until she was moaning. Next I brought my hands into the action, parting the petal lips of her pussy as wide as they'd go, then slurping and sucking at her with my mouth. Jon couldn't get any harder than he already was, but the scene he was watching had to have some effect on him. So, finally, with a guttural moan, he came, shooting deep into my ass and then staying there, his hands holding me tight, fingers slipping beneath my waist to play a magical melody on my clit.

His knowing rhythm brought me up to the ridge of climax, and as Sarah sealed her pussy to my mouth, I found myself coming. Coming between my husband and my friend in the sweetest, stickiest climax of all time. My body was shaking as I worked to keep licking Sarah. I didn't want her to be left out, now that both Jon and I had reached our limits. In no time, Sarah was gripping my shoulders and bucking against my face. She came long and hard, just as Jon had hoped she would, and the way she tasted was so sweet it was almost unreal.

When we were finished, I was dripping from both ends, my mouth slicked up with Sarah's honeyed nectar, my cunt throbbing, Jon's cream dripping out of me. We lay there all together, entwined on the floor of our office, trying to regain our sense of balance, our memory of how to breathe without panting and speak without moaning.

As I stared up at the ceiling, I thought about what Jon must have done. While I was working like a good girl in my office, he'd undoubtedly called Sarah, reminding her that as it was the third Friday of the month, it was his turn to change fantasy into reality. Sarah had taken up her position in the room closest to my office, listening as she waited for the phone call that would beckon her to our house. Listening and stroking herself as the anticipation built inside her.

This meant that next time, Sarah was up. As if reading my mind, Jon leaned forward on one arm and looked over at our sultry neighbor. "Sarah, it's your turn next week. Do you want to play out the rescue fantasy again, or the one where I burst in on you two dirty, naughty coeds?"

"Let's play free-loving freelancers," Sarah said with a smile. "We'll do all the sexy things people think we're doing when we tell them we work at home."

"If they only knew…," Jon and I said together.

Pink Elephants

ERIC WILLIAMS

Don't think about white elephants. Or pink elephants. Or whatever. When someone makes that comment, you just can't help but think about them, right? Enormous, hot pink elephants immediately bebop through your mind. If you were ever in high school band, the parading pachyderms quite possibly will dance in your head to the tune of "The Baby Elephant Walk." Except, this evening, the concept was a little different. Try, "Don't think about getting a hard-on." I mean, don't even fucking think about it. Insert a bitter laugh track here, because, of course—bam. There it is. Mr. Happy. Straight-standing and ready to go.

The main thing to understand is that I had nothing to do with the situation. I wasn't involved in the preparations, didn't plan the outcome. That might sound callous, but it's true. Nora had to understand the full range of possibilities when she brought another girl into the scene. She's aware of my history, of the little nuances that fire those erotic synapses in my fucked-up brain. In fact, she's memorized each and every one of them.

"A slumber party," she said, innocently. "You won't mind, right, Charlie? Me and Reese, hanging out. Watching 'Sex and the City'—" or some other dumb fucking chick show. My mind basically shut down at "slumber party." I could see it all. Tall, blonde, and beautiful Nora and the sleek, dark-haired Reese lounging about our living room in their little see-through nighties, replete with ruffled edges. Or trimmed with marabou fluff straight out of an X-rated, drive-your-man-crazy catalog. I've got a major weakness for feathers.

From the moment she told me that Reese was on the way, I owned instant visions. There they'd be, sitting on our sumptuous gold velvet love seat, drinking some pink frou-frou concoctions, doing their nails or talking about bras. Whatever it is girls do to have fun.

But, really, I didn't have to fantasize too hard about that. I *know* all about what girls do at slumber parties because Nora and I hooked up at one. Got to know each other deep down and personal during the course of a friendly little sleepover. A sleepover in which nobody got any sleep and nobody gave a fuck. At the time, I was dating someone else, an uptight career girl who had a penchant for wearing her hair in a Victorian-style bun. Maybe *uptight*'s not the right word, exactly. "Fully wound" would be a truer description. A serious multitasker, she never really relaxed.

I thought I could melt her. From the first time we met, I had plans of helping her let her hair down—literally. Of spreading her out like some Botticelli model, those loose gingery curls framing her perfect face while I finally changed that serious expression.

That's why I suggested the threesome. I wanted to place her in a lushly decadent position, wanted to see her truly enjoy herself for once. All right, and I'll be perfectly honest here—I wanted to see what her sultry friend Nora looked like beneath her street clothes. Amazingly, it didn't take a lot of convincing before Julia agreed. So maybe she wasn't that uptight after all. Or maybe she was multitasking, once again. Taking care of my needs while exploring her bi-curiosity. And let me tell you, it was amazing. Me and Julia and Nora all spread out on our king-sized bed. Bodies overlapping. Hands busy. Tongues working. Let your mind go. Pink elephants, man, forget that. Try NOT to think about two beautiful women licking each other, topsy-turvy in a sweet sixty-nine. Instant mental picture, right? Instant hard-on.

In the morning, the truth was obvious to all of us. Julia was gay. Nora was into me. And I was in a quandary. What to do? What to do? Move in with the feline blonde with the killer body. That's what I did. And now that same filthy-minded minx was suggesting we do it all over again? Actually, from the sparse amount of information given to me, I couldn't be sure exactly what was on this evening's agenda. And I knew that if I asked—if I put it flat out there on the table and said, "Do I get to fuck Reese, or is this just a girl-girl thing?" well, then I'd look lame, wouldn't I? For not knowing, not having the wherewithal to figure it out for myself.

So, I did what any guy in my position would do. I got a raging hard-on the size of a rocket ship, and I waited impatiently to see what would happen. Waited for Reese to arrive with her little lavender overnight backpack slung innocently over one arm, tripping up our stairs in her high-heeled red gingham slingbacks. Waited hungrily for Nora to offer the invitation, if there was going to be one.

By midnight, I was pretty sure I'd misjudged the party, pretty sure I was going to be spending the night alone in our big bedroom, fulfilling my fantasies with one knowledgeable hand and a bottle of Nora's vanilla-scented body lotion. And that is precisely when my lady strolled down the hall, totally naked, and said, "What are you, crazy? We're *waiting*—"

Still, I could tell from the pleased look in her large gray-green eyes that I'd done the right thing. Behaved like a gentleman. If I'd obviously expected it, or been overly flirtatious with her friend, then she would have dissed me. No pussy for Charlie. But because I'd played it cool, at least on the exterior, I was offered a free pass into heaven. And let me tell you, heaven looks a whole lot like my girl fucking her best friend. With a strap-on.

Nora had the evening well-choreographed. I'll give her that. As soon as I arrived in the living room, I saw the white twisted candles lined up on the mantle, saw our leather sofa bed in place, made up with cherry-pink satin sheets. And Reese, the black-haired vixen, was right in the center of the mattress, glossy burgundy lipstick already slightly smeared around the edges of her full mouth. Some kissing had definitely been going on during the past hour, but I didn't worry myself about that. Girls getting ready. That was all. Of course, Reese was wearing exactly the type of come-fuck-me confection that I'd imagined. Sheer and feather-trimmed. What a knockout.

When she moved, looking over my way, she gave me the kind of dirty wink that would have made me instantly hard on any other occasion. As it was, I just got harder. Staring fixedly at the seductive scene, I stopped at the threshold, knowing that instructions would be forthcoming. Silently, I watched as Nora slid into a dainty leather harness and got on the bed with her buddy. Reese sighed and said Nora's name quietly, reaching forward to trail her fingers over the pink plastic tool before closing her hand tightly around it in a fist.

All right, so I had a moment to wonder how long this evening had been in the works. Nora had to go buy sex toys in preparation for the event. What did that say about my powers of observation? But then I stopped thinking about anything, as I watched my girlfriend play the aggressor in bed. First, she kissed Reese's neck, slowly, lingering as she made her way down her best friend's body. I took a step closer to the bed, wanting to see, wanting to *really* see. Nora pushed that transparent nightie up and out of the way, not bothering to take it off. Little nibbling bites to Reese's nipples made the brunette bombshell moan and toss her head.

Now, we were looking straight into each other's eyes again, and I found I couldn't look away. Not even when Nora continued down the valley of Reese's concave belly to her waiting pussy. Oh, I wanted to watch that. I wanted to observe each motion as Nora parted what I imagined were Reese's plump nether lips and got busy between them, but something happened to me. Rather than lose myself in the pure porno aspect of the evening, I was captivated by the look of unadulterated pleasure in Reese's green-flecked brown eyes. And I just couldn't look away.

"Charlie," she murmured, and I moved even closer, so that we were just one hot breath away from each other, and she reached out and put two fingertips on my bottom lip. Soft, girl fingers rested there so sweetly. I flicked my tongue out to touch them, to draw them into the warmth of my mouth, and I could tell that at this exact moment, Nora began tongue-fucking her. Reese arched her back and her eyes glazed and I couldn't help myself. I leaned forward, cradling her head, wanting to fiercely kiss her, to bite her bottom lip. Necking can be so sexy sometimes. And as Nora continued to play her probe-the-pussy games down there between Reese's lean thighs, I just kissed her friend. Tongues together, breathing meshed. She was so sweet, so ready. And fuck, I could have kissed her for hours.

But Nora had other plans. Sitting up in bed, she slid Reese's legs over her own and plunged inside with her strap-on tool. Reese gasped and pulled away from me, head back on the shiny pillow as Nora brought her hands up to caress her friend's small breasts. Again, I was the observer, and I couldn't tear my eyes from how decadent Reese looked.

"Your cock," she suddenly murmured.

Yeah, my cock. I'd forgotten about it for the moment, but at the words, that thing throbbed hard against my thigh.

"I want it," Reese whispered. Somehow I knew exactly what she meant. She didn't want me to fuck her, because Nora was taking care of that need with perfect ease. She wanted something to suck on. Well, I could help her out. I lost my black boxers in a heartbeat. Climbing onto the mattress, I positioned myself right next to the wild beauty and waited as she turned her head toward me, as she parted those stunning lips and introduced my cock to the warm, wet pleasures within.

And *what* pleasures. Reese had a gentleness to her, a cool quality that had made me peg her in the past as a shy creature. Those large dark eyes, long lashes, sideways glances. But I was wrong. Nothing shy about her. Just a quiet depth, a sweetness to the way she played dirty. With her lips tight around my tool, she sucked hard, and then as she pulled her head back, she carefully grazed my cock with her teeth. Oh, Christ, it felt good, and I pushed against her, wanting more, but she shook her head.

Her speed. Her methods. No pressure.

So I just had to close my eyes and wait. To let her take her time, now licking my balls, moving to get right in there. Making Nora move with her, pulling out and getting behind so that she was taking Reese doggie-style.

Reese looked beautiful. Legs spread, hands steady, holding herself in position as Nora pumped hard inside her, then lifting her head and parting her lips so that she could draw my cock back down her throat. I stroked her soft hair away from her face, staring down at her, seeing that other slumber party in my mind. That night in which Julia had fucked Nora, my lover's hair finally down from that severe style, tickling over her breasts as she gripped Nora's slim waist and ravaged her. Julia had looked the way I'd always imagined she could, untamed and out of control, but as I'd watched her, I'd realized she was looking like that because of someone else. Not me.

Now, Nora was taking over that dominant position, firmly fucking her friend while I got to enjoy the wet wonders of Reese's mouth. She gave Reese a tentative spank on her heart-shaped ass, and I felt the vibrations on my cock as Reese swallowed hard at the sensation. Oh, the girl liked it, and Nora immediately slapped her ass again, leaving a matching pale-purple print on the other side. My cock stirred at that image, because I knew immediately what it would be like to be in Nora's place, taking over the job. Slapping Reese's firm, haughty ass while fucking it. Or even better, I understood what it would feel like to take the luscious raven-haired stunner over my lap, flip up that faux-innocent nightie and give her beautiful bare ass the serious and thorough spanking it deserved.

Yet just as I pictured this, Reese changed the game. She pulled off of Nora, slid back from me, and motioned with her head for me to move.

"What—" I murmured. Then, "Where?"

"Take my spot—"

I wasn't sure. Did she want to watch Nora fuck me? Was I going to like that? But as I hesitated, I saw her slip her delicate fingers over Nora's hips, unbuckling that harness, removing the toy. With calm movements, she strapped the slicked-up tool onto herself, and then waited. Nora and I stared at each other. What was going on? How had Reese so easily managed to usurp Nora's power?

In truth, it didn't really matter how. The intensity was too great to start deciphering the situation, analyzing who should do what to whom and why. We just followed Reese's instructions, Nora taking the spot on her back on the bed and me sliding on top of her, my cock automatically finding its way inside her thrillingly wet pussy. And then Reese—sweet, innocent-looking Reese—was behind me, maneuvering into proper position, her fingertips spreading my muscled asscheeks, trailing down the split between. And then her cock, well-lubed from her own pussy juices, pressed aggressively against my asshole.

Oh, fuck. What was going on?

She slid on in, despite the fact that my body tensed instantly, and that I turned my head to look over my shoulder, wanting to see her face. She just drove forward, as if she'd been ass-fucking men all her life, and I had to take it. Had to, because I wanted it like I'd never wanted anything before. Reese with her rhythm, slip-sliding her way inside me, and me, forgetting who I was or where I was, automatically fucking Nora. Just fucking her. Because I had to.

The three of us, connected—interconnected—worked in synchronicity. Nora, with her eyes shut beneath me, taking the double force of being fucked by two people. Reese would thrust and I would thrust and Nora would groan. Then Reese would pull back, sliding almost all the way out, and I would pull back, so I wouldn't lose contact with her, and Nora would groan again. My mind was filled with gray fog, with white noise. I looked up at the mantle, staring at the candles flickering there, trying to figure out how we'd gotten to this point so quickly.

"Don't try so hard," Reese whispered in my ear, as if she knew exactly what I was thinking. "Don't even try."

Then she ran the tips of her fingers along my shoulder blades and leaned all the way into me, so that I could feel her body pressed along my back. Her breath on the nape of my neck, her mouth opening, teeth searching for purchase on my skin. *Wild thing*, I thought, as she bit me hard. *I guessed wrong. I didn't know.*

What I did know was this: it was only the beginning. This was going to be a long, raucous evening of fun. I saw it all in my mind. But I saw something more. In this position, Nora and I could gaze at each other, and I wondered if she knew what was going to happen. Knew the way I knew.

Because, really, it wasn't my fault. I didn't plan it. Didn't ask to be invited to this bedroom tryst. But in the morning, as Reese packed her tiny nightie away and gave the two of us quick hot kisses good-bye, I understood that I'd be packing soon, as well. That within a week, I'd be at Reese's door, my heart racing as I pictured the way her body would feel next to mine. As I imagined her buckling on a black leather harness, taking me for another ride.

Nora should have known better. Should have understood what it would mean not only to invite a girl into our bed, but into my head.

Pink elephants?

No, man. Just the taste, the glimmer of something new, something that won't let you sleep until you have it again.

The Space Between

HELENA SETTIMANA

I make coffee in my kitchen while the wan light of early morning on the lake filters through the louvers of the Venetian blinds in the cottage. It's the last of my Blue Mountain, a gift from the griot, Kayode "Kayo" Mackenzie of Hilton Head Island. I want it for myself and I fear I'll wake Charmaine, who is still asleep in the loft, and I'll have to share my last drop of him. I roll its liquor on my tongue. Strange that I'd feel that way about something as mundane as coffee, but that's the way it is. It's bitter and sweet; something like the man. Something like all that followed our brief acquaintance. The screen door is squeaky and I try not to let it bang as I step out onto the flagstone patio into the dim morning. The air is fresh, and frosted with the resinous smell of pine, like the interior of a cathedral after mass is said. It is still as a church too, hemmed in by trees some seventy feet tall. It's almost light. Soon the morning chorus will begin. Soon the lake will buzz with boat motors and cries of water-skiers. Soon Charmaine will be getting up, stretching, looking for me.

Last night she lay in the space between my thighs and stabbed at my emptiness with her tongue until it was filled loosely, like water outflowing a cracked vessel. I am empty because she is using me. I know that. I'm using her too. We are like mutually supporting parasites. It's his fault. She is using me because I once had the almost-famous Mackenzie, whom she desires. She has not had the pleasure despite tracking him like a camp follower. Of this I am certain.

"I've been in love with that man for a decade," she confessed over *Cuba Libres* at the old Bam Boo Club in downtown Toronto. Some people idolize singers. Charmaine was like that with poets and artists. So am I, I confess. She responded to Kayo the way women my mother's age swooned over Leonard Cohen. Striped by shade from one of the club's namesake grasses, she swung one sandaled foot under the patio table, her purple-painted toenails coming perilously close to my bare shin. "It's more than lust. It's lo-ove." She flapped her fingers like an excited teenager. I tried not to stare at her cleavage. "I've seen him every time he comes up here. I've even seen him perform *here*," she enthused, waving to take in the whole of the club. "Then I go home and single-handedly console myself that the streets are not paved with talented and handsome men like him, sensitive guys just ripe for the plucking. Any girl should get one. But no," she sucked her teeth, "those ones are rare and worth the wait, not that a girl should go without some while she is waiting."

We laughed, but I was a bit put out. I wished she wasn't

so transparently smitten, even if I agreed wholeheartedly with her assessment of Kayo's worth. A girl shouldn't go without a bit of something. I could be that something for her. Like Charmaine, I'm in love with words and most recently with her words. My guru says I shouldn't trust what people say, only what they do, but I'm susceptible to art and sweet talk. I'd been working at bedding Charmaine for six months now, ever since the writers' conference where we met. She's brilliant—a poet as well. I'm a sucker for that sort of shine; that sort of smart-hot. She had always been willing to come out to talk, to shop or share, but I'd wanted more for a long time. I searched her face and the shifting plains and hills of her body for clues, but had found no evidence of my desire returned. That she was so indifferent to me hurt. She thrummed with passion. I quivered back. She was edible. I was hungry. I stared across the table. She looked away. She had broad, high cheekbones, a diamond-shaped face that spoke of her jambalaya roots: Trini, French, Indian, African. Creole. Red. Her eyes were large, and the corners curled down slightly. This was beautiful. But it was her body; the queenly heft of it, and the way she moved her high chest and broad behind with grace upon slender legs like stalks of grass that I found so compelling. Her ass jutted one way, her tits, belly and chin the other, like those African carvings of dancing girls with long shins and a hand on one hip. That and the words. The words.

We were talking American poets. Slammers. The import Dub set. Spoken-word traditionalists. That's her thing. She brought up Kayo's name and I sat for a long time contemplating my drink and the plate of over-sour escoveitched snapper steaming in front of me. In this moment I sensed a shift about to occur, some rending of the fabric of my universe. "I know him," I said, finally, "personally...."

She looked at me with surprise.

"How come you never said so? No. Don't shit me."

"I guess it never occurred to me. We had an affair a year ago."

She weighed this statement against what she believed. "No. No way...he'd never. He's a separatist. He's all for *la raza,* Leni."

I shrugged, burning inwardly. Truth was often stranger than art. We invent some of our truths. I couldn't keep my trap shut. Fuck her if she thought I couldn't be telling the truth because he was out there saying he wouldn't touch whitey. There I was, shoving one sacred cow in her face. I wished to fuck she wanted me. There, take that. I attempted the fish. The vinegar rankled in my nostrils and burned my tongue. I pushed it away, called the waiter and asked to see the menu again....

"Well, he did. We did. The only thing he was separating then were my legs. Not long, not deep...not love I'm afraid...." She stared at me, disbelieving. "I met him in Charleston. I was doing that article for *Saturday Night.* I have some pictures. Maybe I'll show you. You can come over."

I did have pictures; there was not much to divine from them. They didn't show us, or anyone else fucking. But there is always a story behind an image. In my favorite, he is standing on a narrow, cobbled lane in Charleston, under a huge hanging fern, his bald head turned to one side, his cheek laid across one shoulder. The flash glints off of one earring, dangling along his cheek. The fern stands on the side of his head, looking like a great green jester's cap; a woodland king's crown, sliding off. A church spire rises in the distance at the end of the alley. He is smiling, gap-toothed, goofily at the camera. That was the day after we met. We'd shared breakfast without touching.

I'd been pulled by a bill posted on a telephone pole to attend a slam of Island poets in a backstreet club. I thought, *great,* I could do an extra article on contemporary Gullah culture alive and well in South Carolina. It's why I was there, after all—dredging stories. I went into that place, shining like the North Star. It was fantastic: hot, angry, exuberant. There was much shouting and later, pressing of flesh, the knocking of knuckles in acknowledgment of the groove. I was talking to the performers and he, sliding past my table after his set, did a double take and asked if I had got lost. I laughed and said no. He was very tall, and dark like espresso, with a split in his smile that made him look like an overgrown boy. I was not lost. I was there for the show. Spur of the moment, I asked if I could interview him. He sat down and talked, and that was the beginning. He said to come for breakfast at his hotel. What the hell…I did. We drove in his old truck to the Island, after.

Some men are so facile with their charm they astound me. I love that much moxie. He asked. I went. Simple. His sunglasses made him look professorial. He smiled a tiny, tiny inscrutable smile the whole way. We didn't talk on the drive. Not much. I mouthed some appreciation of the raw power of his words. He waxed philosophical and stressed how important his work is to the culture of the Island. The ego—but I got that he wasn't making it up. I suggested we save it for the interview proper. Pausing in speech, he had the distracting habit of touching his tongue to his upper lip. It made my insides twitchy. I looked out the window. I watched his hands, slid my eyes to the side and examined his belly; the tented folds of his loose trousers. If I wasn't conscious of it before, I acknowledged it now: I'd sleep with him, should that occasion arise.

We stopped for groceries. The clerk eyed me with some interest and looked pointedly at Mackenzie, but he offered no explanation of my presence. When we left, I felt the cashier's eyes on my back and didn't turn around.

He stayed on the Island in a beach house, where the ocean raced up to meet the land, and the wind battered the thin grass flat. Sandpipers raced ahead of the surf and chased it back as it sucked in upon itself, sighing. They peeped as they ran. Palmettoes spiked the grainy ground around the house. I thought it was a miracle the place still stood, a survivor of countless storms. The pale yellow paint peeled on the clapboard. I walked up the tall steps, the house high on its pilings, its hedge against the cruelty of the sea. A pelican stood on the roof. I stood outside for several minutes before stepping in.

"Y'all like hush puppies?" he called from the bright kitchen. It was a blaze of sunflower gold.

"Sure. I'll eat anything."

"Greens?"

"Anything, honestly."

"Fried clams?"

"Sure."

"Well if you want 'em y'all'll have to get 'em. There's a pail and a digger out on the porch. Go get us some, then. Know how to find 'em, right?" I nodded. "Make sure you bring 'em in some clean water. Tide's out so it's perfect. They'll be frisky, though. Work fast. See if you can find some crabs, too."

I was back in half an hour, the bucket filled. He puttered in the kitchen, pots clattering, conversing as he worked, and emerged shortly with two steaming plates, topped with sliced tomatoes, dusted with pepper and parsley.

Over lunch and for part of the afternoon, I asked the questions, got my answers, sipped on the Bud he'd pulled out of the fridge.

"Ya'll are welcome to stay and I can drive you back in the morning or whenever y'all have to get back. Nothin' ever happens out here, anyway. They be talking about you back at the store. That's how dull it is in this part. I c'n hear 'em talk about how y'all got lost from the other side. Should be with the country-club folk." He laughed. "Should keep them going for a while. Might as well give 'em something more to talk about. Besides, it looks like the day is turning rough. Check it out." He pointed out to the darkening sea.

A squall had blown up offshore and the surf rose with the tide until water licked close to the verandah's stilted legs.

"Shouldn't we be getting away?"

"Nah. Seen worse 'an 'at. Not likely going to go higher than 'at, and there's a spot down the road a ways where there's more chance of a washout than here. Might not get past that point, anyway. Might as well stay and enjoy the show. It's best if you get out on the porch an' stick ya head into the wind. Always makes me feel like a sea captain. A reg'lar pirate." His twin earrings shook.

So we stood on the porch while the waves sucked at the ground and the rain sliced and swung like a curtain parted and swaying upon itself. It turned and drove itself into us like needles. A huge explosion of lightning made me jump, crashing into him, sodden. We scurried back inside.

"Damn." He was laughing, a big boom, boom, boom of a laugh like thunder.

"I feel like a drowned rat…."

"Y'all look like one, too, sorry to tell ya. I'll fetch you a towel and if you like I can throw your stuff over the drying rack. I'll getcha something dry to wear."

He came back with a huge towel and a sweatshirt, then passed me some flannel pajama bottoms with a drawstring waist. "You can change in the bathroom or the bedroom, wherever you like."

"Thanks." I chose the bath, took some time drying my hair. When I came back out, I found him standing in the same place, but dressed in a floor-length plain linen caftan. Barefoot. He looked like a prince. Like Fishburne in *Othello*…. He was smoking a joint.

"Y'okay?"

"Yeah," I said. "Thanks." I handed him my wet things. He put them on the table and turned back to me.

"You want some?"

"Sure," I said, holding out my hand. "Sure. Love to."

"You need more research for your article?"

"I'm always open for new information."

"What do you need?"

"I don't know what else to ask. So I'll just remain open."

Lightning blued the light in the room.

"You want an exclusive?" That funny smile I'd seen in the truck reappeared.

"Like what? I thought I already had one." He touched his tongue to his lip, again. I passed the joint back, sputtered a little. He put it down. And he kissed me. "Oh," said I. A peck behind the ear, a suggestion laid upon the nape of my neck, an invitation pressed to my lips, an invocation upon my tongue. We stood like that for a long time, tasting. I mouthed his neck, at this darker hollow in a dark hollow near the collar bone. In that spot the smell of salt and wind was strong. I licked it. Salty, too—sweat and sea spray.

"Shoulda jus' given you the towel," he said.

I stroked him through his robe, testing weight, length, breadth and started to feel giddy at the thought of slowly jerking this man off through what looked like an exotic housedress. Was that all I'd do? Maybe he would just want to be sucked. My legs wobbled. Where would this end? The kitchen table? The paneled wall of the den? Domestically in bed, missionary style?

"Leni, are you in there?" She kicked me on the shin. Charmaine was looking at me. I snapped back to the present. The Bam Boo's purple-haired waitress hovered.

"Yeah…just thinking about what you said. You're gonna have to take my word for it. I did. We did. He's not entirely who you think he is. Who he says he is."

After our lunch, Charmaine came over to my house for the first time. I showed her the pictures.

Proof. Sort of.

"Damn, I could just kill you. I'm so jealous I could spit."

"Well, get over it—it's not like I married the guy. He was very cool. He was fulla himself, though. A regular cock of the walk...but he was...," I sighed, "...for two days he was the finest man I ever was with. Sometimes I get mad, thinking about it. You know, you have the fling and it gets under your skin. You want more and it's not there."

"Please put me out of my misery and tell me about it...."

"About what?"

"About it all...his cock. What he said... Sometimes I read his poetry and I start thinking stuff...and I want to put it there...."

"Oh girl, you have it bad," I said. I felt that shift again, the rip in the universe. If I let something go, I might get what I craved. But should I? I wasn't the kiss-and-tell sort. Still, this could be my ticket. She wouldn't touch me. Fuck it.

So I told her. I told her everything. She *so* wanted to know. I tormented her. I told her about lifting the linen robe very slowly, until it bunched over the high curve of his ass, held there by my fist; how his cock drizzled wet across my rib cage. Her mouth fell open, her lips wet, wet, wet, too. Looking into her mouth I remembered taking him in mine, the smell of salt marsh and wet earth, the clay tang of him as his wrinkled sheath rolled back and my tongue snaked around him, his hands in my hair. This, I told her. With her next exhalation, I was back sprawled on his sofa, exulting in his tongue parting my lips, and his words, "You taste like the sea," eddying over me as he dragged my clit between his gapped teeth and tortured it slowly with the very same clever, pink source of all that jive that had sprung from his mouth. "I'm floating on your sea...." And at this her mouth dropped open again, and in it I saw desire, and I leaned forward and put my mouth on hers, and said, "This is how it all went down...." On her, I redrew the map—rewrote the history of that travel. The key to this had been so simple, and so unfair to use.

She writhed on the couch beside me, ripe, like a mashy Mission fig—soft. I stroked the narrow silk gusset of her panties, slick already. She was unfashionably and beautifully unshorn, a dense mat of hair peeping all around, spreading to her upper thighs, up the inner cheeks of her ass, the indigo ribbon of her lips glistening then parting slightly: pink, like conch, inside, a recollection of the sea.

I whispered how, for all the gushing wet pouring out of me, he still hurt me with his thing. How it took working slowly, until he said, "Pull the skin fo'ward," and then pushed into me in one slick motion. Farting and sucking from my stretched insides, gales of air caught and released. I bunched my fingers, two, three at a time, into her. She mewled. I pushed, felt resistance, pushed again and again until my hand was clenched around its breadth by her gaping mouth and she broke like surf on it. "Like that," I said. "Big, just like that, Charm. I was bent over the windowsill, with my face in the glass, facing the storm, the rain pelting the window, running down the glass. He made me shoot. That never happened before. It hasn't happened since."

Charmaine grasped my hand, shuddered, jerked like a spastic or a Voudoun in trance, babbled in a strange tongue like that of love; then cried, hiccoughing into my chest.

Later I made her some of the coffee he'd given me; a gift in parting. One of his friends fronted him the expensive Jamaican grind. The stuff cost a fortune. I kept it, sealed in my fridge. Rationed it.

We smoked one too, and I petted her hair, twisted the ends and rewrapped the scarf around it so it stood up in spikes like dragons' tongues. She looked like a queen. She checked my work in the mirror, and was surprised. "You did a good job."

"I have hidden talents." We laughed.

I haven't seen Kayo since that time. A year. We keep missing each other. I'm always where he's not. I don't feel like I'm entirely done. Like the poor SOB jonesing twenty minutes after his first stem of rock, I'm not done. It keeps me on edge. Moist and restless.

I can hear her stirring upstairs. The place is already beginning to heat up. It will be a clear, calm day, perfect for summer idling. I know that part of the past is why she continues to see me, sometimes calling in the night for a fix. We keep apart unless it's to fuck, or in this case to flee into the country. Anais and June... Much as I'd like to, I can't call it making love. We'd have to be in love with each other. Seems we're both in lust with him. It's not a fair trade. We don't talk about him, either. That would be too much an acknowledgment of this two-sided triangle. Kayo's the lacuna, the space between, the spirit in the bed. That's my dry, hollow place. If I shut my eyes I'll allow her to be my diviner and I'm her channeler, her shaman. The water flows from the cracked pot, out of the space within its walls. I talk to her. I know the words. Blunt. My fist is his cock—my tongue is his too. It fills her gap. I know what it felt like. I can take her there—almost. I wish it were enough. One day I might have to deal with her finding him herself, except not by accident. She'll go looking.

Then, I don't know what will happen. Sometimes I wish I hadn't told her, but in this game the end justifies the means. It's what I dealt for.

In the meantime we revolve about each other in an uneasy orbit, listening to the loons laugh like unhinged spirits on the lake. Pretending. I make her herb tea. I must make a trip into town to get some coffee. I'm out.

Harvest Time

SASKIA WALKER

"Take me to bed," Ash rasped against her hair, clutching at her.

"And me," Joel growled, pressed against the other side, the three of them clinging together, breathless and panting, in the gloom of the hallway. Joolz threw back her head, laughing joyously, reveling in the sensations. They had chased each other back across the moonlit fields and tumbled into the cottage in the early hours, giddy after a night of festivities unique to Dorset villages in harvest time.

She dropped her sandals from her hand and led them to the large bedroom, peeling off her dress as she went. It was still hot, even though it was so late; it was easily one of the hottest summers she could remember.

"I'm sticky as hell; I'm going to take a shower," she said.

Joel threw himself into a chair, ruffling his hand through

his spiky black crop, eyeing her hungrily. Ash, lean and fair, with a goatee and shaggy hair, lounged on the bed, arms behind his head, watching her through narrowed eyes as she dropped the dress on the floor and then turned away into the adjacent bathroom.

Joolz smiled at her reflection in the bathroom mirror as she flicked on the shower, enjoying the anticipation that had hummed between them all evening. The three college friends had fallen into a relationship quite casually, a few weeks earlier. First Ash and Joolz had become lovers, and then one night Joel had been with them, and he'd stayed and he'd kissed her while Ash fucked her. She'd put her hand on Joel's cock, jerking him off, and it had sent Ash wild. That night he gave her the best fuck she'd ever had, rutting at her like a wild man.

After that, the three of them hung out together even more, constantly wired for sexual suggestion. Sometimes the men took her one after the other; sometimes she liked to watch one man wanking, while the other fucked her. The two men let Joolz determine the mechanics of their relationship. That made her smile; they didn't like that kind of responsibility, but she did, so it was a very satisfactory arrangement. Joolz enjoyed the power. She also enjoyed slowly upping the ante between them.

She soaped her breasts under the lukewarm water, smiling as she thought back to the image of the men in the pub, how lean and gorgeous they looked alongside the beefier farm workers. The two men noticed when other men looked at her, their gaze darting and suggestive. Ash seemed to take a perverse kind of enjoyment from sharing her with Joel, and it made him want her in a very forceful, physical way. Seeing Ash get territorial and act on it made Joel hot. He told them it was like watching a live sex show of his very own. And Joolz? Joolz simply enjoyed each and every experience the dynamic between them offered.

That evening, while a fiddler played in the snug, and skittles led the gambling in the main bar, they had both held her and kissed her. Amidst the celebrations of fecund mother earth, it was as natural an occurrence as the rising of the seasons. The three London socialites had found that the traditions of the countryside inspired something even more earthy and real, something entirely unashamed. They had claimed her as theirs, publicly.

Joolz flicked her hair back as she climbed out of the shower, glancing around at the old bathroom walls, remarking to herself how well the place had stood up to time. She hadn't been back to the rambling cottage for four years, even though it remained in the family after Grandma had passed on and was always on offer for holidays. It was the place where she had spent her childhood summers and big family celebrations at Christmastime and other special times, she reflected. She'd slept with Laurence, here. He was her first lover. She glanced back at the mirror, remembering. Her dark eyes turned black, her mouth opening as thoughts spiraled in her mind. Back then she'd been eager, but jittery. Now, she looked ripe, ready. After a few moments, she lifted her kimono from the back of the bedroom door and slipped it on.

A wedge of moonlight carved into the room from the open curtains. They were both sitting on the bed, expectantly. They looked at her body through the flimsy silk kimono she had thrown on. It was sheer and clung to her damp skin. She shook her head and her long chestnut hair tumbled over her shoulders, damp from the shower.

"You look nubile, half undressed in the moonlight," Joel said from the bed, smirking as he pulled his T-shirt over his head. Joolz smiled and wandered toward them. She crept up from the bottom of the bed to lie between them.

"That's funny that you said that, you know," she mused. "Because I had just remembered that I lost my virginity in this very room."

"Mmm, Joolz. You say all the right things." Joel rolled closer and lifted up on his elbow, moved his mouth to her earlobe and kissed it, his hand stroking over her breast.

"Really?" Ash asked, looking at her with curiosity. "Tell us about it...," he prompted. She smiled. It turned him on, big-time, when she talked about sex. He put one hand on her thigh, gently enclosing its curve of flesh as he climbed next to her. Joel began to unbutton his jeans, kicking them off.

"I was seventeen. It was a colleague of my father's, Laurence. I haven't seen him in years." Her mind drifted back and forth, riding the time between then and now. "I'd been infatuated with him for an age. He was well aware of it and he—well, he pursued me." She gave a light laugh.

"That's understandable," Joel said. "The guy obviously had good taste." He chuckled, kissing her silk-draped breast. She covered his head with her hand, stroking his hair.

"Go on," Ash said, his eyes dark with lust and a spark of something else—envy? Joolz lifted her eyebrows at him, a teasing smile lifting the corners of her mouth.

"He had just come back from Nepal, where he had been writing a travel journal. I was swept up in the visions he described during dinner. At the end of the evening, when I left, he kissed my hand. Deliberately. It made me feel like a woman,

I suppose. The second night of his visit, he retired early and when I went to bed, I found him in the corridor. He caught me in his arms and put his fingers to his lips. Then he pulled me in here." Joolz glanced round the room. Joel was kissing her shoulder; tiny light nibbles, just anchoring her.

"He asked me questions about my sexual desires, and I told him about the strange tugging that I felt, every night, the unfulfilled lust, deep inside. He began to stroke my body, slowly taking my clothes off."

Joel moved against her, his body responding to her comments. She felt his hard outline against her thigh. Her sex had begun to cloy with need, need inspired by real sensation, and memory.

"Then he began describing what it felt like, for him, wanting me...he told me he wanted to push his cock deep inside me. His fingers were all over my underwear, pulling it off me. I could barely breathe." Joolz paused. Ash had risen and stripped of his shirt, baring the strong lean muscle of his chest. She linked one finger over the belt on his jeans, tugging it open. She looked up at him, provocatively as she popped open the buttons on his fly.

"He explored me thoroughly with his fingers; all I could do was let the experience eat me up—his eyes were so inquisitive on my virgin flesh. But I wanted him to look at me...." She drew his cock out, embracing it firmly as it grew harder in her hand. He groaned, his body wavering.

"I want to look at you, now," Joel commanded, his hand roving up her thigh. Ash reached over and stopped him.

"Let her finish," he whispered, through clenched teeth. The hunger had bitten him. Joolz smiled but looked away as he stripped and lay back against her again, his body taut with lust.

"I was a bit…scared—when he undressed, and I saw his cock. I hadn't seen a real man naked before…only pictures." Ash jammed his cock against her side, his eyes glazed, his features contorted with restraint. She squirmed against him; he locked one hand over her hip, holding her against his pulsing cock. "He led me to the bed and spread my legs wide." She gestured toward the end of the bed, her feet sliding against each other as she saw herself there.

"He kissed me down there first, not deeply…like you do…" She paused to stroke Joel's head again. He muzzled against her. "…but enough to make me whimper. When he touched me inside, I thought I would die. It was excruciating, but so good! Then, his cock…it felt huge, so huge. I wondered how I could ever manage it, but at the same time, I wanted to impale myself on it. To have it thrust—thrust right through me."

Joel groaned, his body writhing alongside hers, his hand lifting open her kimono, stroking her bare legs. She opened them in response.

"Touch me," she said, turning to him. His fingers slid against the wetness of her sex.

"Go on," Ash murmured, his body extending itself against hers, his mouth against her neck. "Don't stop." His erection was rigid. He pressed it against her thigh. Joolz gasped, completely aware of the male forces surrounding her, and still picturing herself spread-eagled on the bed, breathless and afraid, taking the huge cock inside her for the first time. She closed her eyes and let the feeling of Joel's fingers questing through her wetness take her back again. She wanted penetration.

"I wanted—penetration. I wanted it, but it also terrified me. When he began to take me I thought my body would break, he seemed so huge. But, God, it felt good!"

Joel rammed his fingers inside her; she gasped, and then began to move on them, her head falling back, her body sliding down against the bed.

"He fucked me so hard, mercilessly."

Ash knelt up, dragged her legs wider apart, and climbed between them. He pulled Joel's hand away from her, his cock quickly finding the wet niche between her legs. Joolz cried out, a muted scream, as he thrust inside her.

"Shut up!" he ordered. "Not another word." His body drew back and reached. He was wild; it was as if he was suddenly furious at her words, and at the heat she was giving off. "Don't say another word, Joolz." He gritted his teeth as he thrust inside her. Oh, that was good. A demon sprang up inside her.

"Harder than that... Ash, he rode me harder than that." She held him with her eyes, urging him on, matching the challenge in her words. He rode up against her, thrusting repeatedly, more quickly, fiercely. Joolz was swept up into his rhythm, molten inside, sensitized to every movement.

Ash thrust faster, rose up on his arms, and then freed a bitter cry of anger in his throat as his cock came suddenly, spurting into her. He had barely slowed his movement before Joel was there, ready to take her from him. Joolz felt a rush of departure, and then she was filled again. Two cocks, she was having two cocks, one after the other. God, that was good. The men with her and those in her memory a multitude of pleasures, already she was blossoming into orgasm. Her pelvis was awash with heat, her body shuddering.

"I want more," she cried out. Joel swore under his breath and fucked her harder, even while she was still clutching him.

"You look so bloody hot when you come," Joel whispered. Her core pounded, waves of relief washing over her.

"I want more," she cried out again, delirious with pleasure. Her eyes flickered open when she heard Ash's voice.

"Don't come, hold up," he said, his hands on Joel's shoulders. Joel swore again, louder. The physical effort of halting, when every atom in his body wanted to go on, demanded all his efforts. Ash was standing beside the bed, fisting his cock, which was already long and hard again, ready for more. "She said she wants more, she wants more cock." Ash's eyes were flashing. Joel pulled out for a moment. Holding his aching balls tight, he sat back onto his haunches, pressing against the base of his cock to hold back from coming. Ash moved closer, offering his cock to her. Joolz turned her face into it. Oh, yes. She wanted to feel it fill her mouth; she wanted to taste his passion.

"Do you still want more?" Ash asked her, his voice controlled. Joolz groaned, her body ricocheting with a riot of opposing signals; she was unable to form words. "Yes?" he murmured, and she nodded her head, her hair trailing over her face as she swayed, intoxicated with it, overwhelmed with shame, shame that flooded her sex when she was forced to concede that she did want more.

"Yes, two cocks, I want you to fill me up," she blurted out, moving round so that her head was hanging back at the edge of the bed, opening her mouth to him.

"Sweet Jesus," Joel said, pressing harder still.

Ash's cock was close to her lips, still slick and oozing, a

drop of come weeping out onto the swollen dark-red head. He drew back and Joolz cried out, grabbing at him, thrusting him into her mouth, suckling hard. He stood directly behind her and slid deep against her throat with each slide in and out of her mouth. Joolz wanted it, but she wondered if she could take it without gagging, if she could breathe at all. Then she found her rhythm, swallowing a good length of him and an intake of breath on each of his thrusts. She felt Joel's hands on her again, urgent, and the nudge of his cock in her sex. She wanted this so badly, she wanted to be filled and used, to be taken every way, so full of cock that every ounce of her was going to be drenched with come.

"That's it," Ash whispered, panting. "Oh, yes, you're so good at that, baby." He rubbed his hand over her breasts, examining her, his fingers hard against her peaked nipples. Joolz felt feverish, weak, and agitated all at the same time. She was so thoroughly pinioned and exposed. Waves of sensation skittered over her whole body. It felt thoroughly debauched, but right and true, as if being subdued and penetrated by them both like that was what her body craved in that moment. She felt like mother earth herself, rooted through and penetrated with virile roots spilling their seed on her land. Her body went limp, malleable, absorbing each wave of sensation. She began to come again, very quickly, her body lifting up, her sex clenching and spasming.

Ash grunted, his body gleaming with sweat and taut with effort, his hips rolling. Joel was panting, his cock rock-hard, at its most swollen as it finally shot its load. Ash cursed loudly, then his cock began to jerk: once, twice, three times, giving her the taste of him, before he pulled out, still spurting furiously over her neck and breasts. He leaned over her, panting, and when she caught her breath again, she pulled him down onto the bed with them, dizzy with pleasure.

"Enough cock, Madame?" he asked, his voice edged with sarcasm.

"Enough—for now," she retorted.

"You're insatiable," Joel murmured, collapsing back on the bed.

"Not with you two around." She chuckled.

"Well, if this Laurence friend of yours should drop 'round," Ash mused, as he lay down and kissed her forehead affectionately. "I think we should tie you to the bed and show him how to really fuck a woman."

"Oh, now there's an idea," Joolz said, smiling. She had to admit, the suggestion fascinated her. "But he might just drop 'round anytime, so you should get ready to act on that threat of yours."

Ash's head jerked up and he looked at her possessively. Joolz raised her eyebrows at him, hauling him closer.

"Just teasing."

"Sure you are," he replied, and they looked into each other's eyes, the suggestion he had made taking root. With Joel at her back, the three of them began to drift toward sleep, limbs entwined, sticky, and happily sated. For now. Joolz smiled to herself; tomorrow she might just have to up the ante again. One important lesson that she had learned from the countryside was that if you made your hay while the sun shined, then you were sure to be kept well stocked, and satisfied, all year around.

Craving Faces
TOM PICCIRILLI

Sometimes you just want to go home and toss in a horror DVD—*Bride of Re-Animator* or something by Fulci, *The Beyond* maybe—page through a men's mag and check out the latest articles on who was out there getting laid, what the new scene was, where it could be found, who painted themselves with liquid latex in the clubs you could never find, whatever the hell was happening in the heartland.

But no matter how hard you try to skip out of work early, they get you in a hammerlock and hang you up for an extra ninety minutes.

So I was trapped at the office for the duration, on the Friday before Thanksgiving, caught right at the crux of holiday rush hour. There was no point in getting on the expressway because I'd just as soon relax in a McDonald's for the evening sipping coffee than sit in my overheating car trapped in gridlock, feeling my pulse bust one-fifty.

I got some fast food, read the paper, and people watched, staring at the upper-middle-class teenagers acting loud and funky, talking white-bread trash like they were ghetto rappers who'd come up off the streets.

Joy walked in about then. She temped for the office where I worked, and was polite without being amiable. Midtwenties, draping bangs of black hair, young but with something of an old school punk attitude. She had a mouth that was a little too large for her elfin face, and I found it arousing, those lips shining under the harsh lights. She had her entire upper left arm covered in tattoos of roses, scowling eyes, and distorted mutant children. One other design sort of peeked out from around the top button of her blouse. I couldn't figure out what it might be.

"Hi Joy," I said and motioned her to sit with me.

She didn't. She stood beside my table and quietly said, "Hello," in such a way that I realized she didn't even know my name. It made me a touch pissy and kind of curious, wondering why I didn't rate enough to make an impression. Sometimes you found your pride when you least wanted the damn thing.

We chatted for a few minutes and bored each other to shit. She seemed filled with a nervous energy that bled through and nearly brushed me back in my seat. Her eyes were dark and brimming with an intensity and eagerness, and prodded me in all the right places and some of the wrong ones too. I couldn't be certain if it was a sexual tension, but I sure was hoping.

"Would you like to go somewhere for a drink?" I asked.

It was a loser's play, really, thinking you could just calmly drift from McDonald's to some quaint blues bar, but suddenly I felt each minute of my life being wasted. The thought caused an abrupt sense of dismay to lurch inside me.

Joy shrugged and the motion tossed a handful of hair over one eye. She appeared quite aware of each one of her gestures, their inherent cuteness, as if somebody had commented on them all at one time or another. Her grin was bright but sorrowful, and it stopped me.

She said, "I've got a full plate of double death-by-chocolate cake out in my car. I brought it for a friend's baby shower this morning. I didn't realize it was poor etiquette to offer a pregnant woman something so fattening, and I got reamed for it. Want a piece?"

"Sure."

Leading me with the angle of her jaw, she directed me through the parking lot to a red vintage '64 Chevy Impala that had seen a lot of miles and fender benders. But it was still a classic ride, and I was soon tapping into the Americana road myth of my youth, imagining myself behind the wheel, the hum of the asphalt vibrating up through the steering column, a gorgeous girl beside me as we swung from town to town.

The Chevy took up three spots in the back parking lot by the dumpsters, tail end huge enough to fit a family of six. I started getting into the passenger side when she folded the seat down and slid in back. I got in with her feeling the charged possibility of the moment growing thicker, already smelling chocolate and my own rising sweat.

We sat on the bench like two kids waiting for their parents to take them to church. She handed me a closed cake box and I held the thing without any idea of what to do with it.

On the page it would've been different. Standing in a bar at midnight we could've spoken about all the meager goals that stung the back of our skulls, but now I'd about lost every ounce of my cool. No slickness in the least, and she picked up on it. I wondered if we'd ever get a chance to talk literature, European art, the burning world of everything we hated and prized. The McDonald's coffee had thrown me off my game.

She said, "You're getting upset. Am I making you nervous?"

"It's not that exactly. It's just—"

"We're not on a date. Not in a sports bar. And this isn't a candlelit restaurant or the office. So you're not sure how to act."

"Essentially."

She smiled, the wide mouth easing back and back, those lips arching. "You always feel the need to put things in their proper places, in a nice matching order?"

"I was toilet trained at eighteen months," I told her.

"My, you have a lot to be proud of."

Sometimes you know you're being a whole lot more ignorant than you should be. I turned to stare at her, still holding the cake. What the hell was I doing holding cake? Why'd she have cake in the back of her car anyway? Who brings cake to a baby shower?

Christ, on occasion the simple became nothing but nonsense. Joy smiled and let out a soft chuckle, and I understood she'd been playing me a touch, which was fine. She had it all over me.

I tossed the box down and felt the sudden burn in my guts and in my brain, the wanting of her now when I didn't much care a minute ago. Maybe it was the laugh that did it. Maybe I just wanted to see those tattoos up close.

She noticed that I was looking and said, "Don't be shy."

"I'm not," I said. "I want to watch for a moment."

"Yes, you can do that," she breathed and I leaned forward and ran my tongue over her neck, up across that lengthy jawline as she groaned. "I want your attention."

There it was, our relationship established. The sound caught me good and low like a serrated blade and raised my cock to three-quarters mast. She knew it too and placed her hand on my inner thigh, casually brushing her fingers over my trousers from side to side until I was completely erect.

And I knew she didn't want me, but instead wanted something from me. I was there for her, and it tripped me up for a second, but the heat was on the back of my neck. She gave that condescending giggle again and I grunted in frustration. Joy undid my pants, unzipped me and stared at my tented shorts, pinching her chin, inspecting.

"Come on," I urged.

"Beggar," she said.

"Hell yeah."

"But you haven't begged enough." Not cutting, but with a lightly irritated tone.

"I'm great at whining."

"I bet you are."

She pulled the waistband down. My cock bobbed forth and she knelt over me.

It wasn't a subservient position. She was in complete control and knew it. I looked out the back window at the folks heading to the drive-up window. Nobody noticed us. I sprang to full attention, thrust toward her mouth. She contemplated my body and took time to examine my cock carefully. She touched the head softly, using her thumb and forefinger to pluck a drop of precum away. I shrugged out of my shirt and kicked off my pants. I let out a snarl like an angry dog, and maybe I was one just then. Maybe always.

"You don't run the show," she said.

"What?"

"You like to be in control. Little boys who are potty trained at eighteen months are disciplined and like to be in command."

"Uh, hey now, not necessarily."

"Or do you like to be controlled?"

She rubbed the tender meaty ridge and brought her lips low, nibbling at it. I wanted her to gobble me but she had a hint of the tease to her and kept toying, making me writhe. She drew her tongue along the reddish pink ring directly under the head of my cock, her bottom teeth scraping gently.

Twinges shot up into my belly and I had to shift again, an animal loose in my throat.

She held on tightly and whispered, "No, you won't get away, unless I want you gone."

"I…know." I always did.

"You do, don't you?"

"Uh-huh," I breathed between clenched teeth. Joy opened that lusciously large mouth once more, and I gasped as she took me in. She threaded her fingers through my pubic hair and clutched at it, tugging too hard until I snorted and then she tenderly smoothed it out. She tapped her fingers against my nutsack, bobbling it in her hand as she sucked me harder.

The edges of my vision melted into white light. She let my cock slip from her lips and pressed her face into my crotch, breathing in the musk of my groin. I grabbed the edges of those funky bangs and parted them to view her forehead, where all the thunderstorms happened. She seemed drunk from the heady scent, or maybe it was only the power over a mostly simple man. She carefully hefted my balls and slid first one and then both into her mouth.

Her tongue darted back to the head of my cock and I shivered and snorted while the loudspeaker squawked *Can I take your order?* Monotonous voices ordered happy meals, no cheese, extra fries, apple pies.

Seizing my shaft Joy started jerking me harder, slapping my cock against her cheek as she made eye contact and grinned up at me. It got the tickle going, and I thought I might cum right then, but she instantly stopped and left me on the fence, in pain and thrashing from pleasure.

Freakin' A right I didn't run the show. She said, "I'm doing this because I want to, do you understand?"

"Sure."

"Good. I wish this." She tantalized me and giggled, and after I'd calmed, she let my cock graze her chin again. I shoved forward, fucking her mouth while she took it, and then her hands reached over and she exerted a pressure on my hips, holding me down.

"Not too fast," she said.

Goddamn. Joy let her top hang off her shoulders for an instant, exposing her tits and showing me they were much larger than I'd expected. 38C or thereabouts, with huge pink aureoles the size of half dollars, nipples perked but not jutting.

Blooming across her entire left breast was the face of a woman, painted mouth slightly open as if in the middle of a whisper.

They were Joy's features, but not quite.

The artwork was too intricate, far too realistic, to be just a stranger. So I gave in and asked, "Who is it?"

"Me," she said.

"No."

"The geek set down in the skin."

"The hell's that mean?"

She didn't offer any explanation, and I wasn't sure I really wanted to hear one, especially then. It was strange, lying there, having both of them watching me.

She didn't even slow down as she took the rest of her clothes off, slipping them down and around her body like a dancer drawing veils. "Come in my mouth. In mine and in hers."

"Jesus, lady."

Joy drew aside her panties and hiked her knees up. I wanted to go down on her but there wasn't enough room and I was already detonating with need. I leaned into her, plunging my cock in so easily that it almost startled me. She was so wet that I felt drops of her come splash up against my public hair.

"That's it," she whispered.

"God, yes."

She kept our movements slow, rocking lightly as I pushed harder. She was wonderfully tight and had great muscular control, tensing and loosening around me. She gasped as I kept fucking her, finding the rhythm and enjoying how her tits bounced each time I rammed her. I got to that good place where, for maybe ten seconds, I wasn't thinking of a damn thing and had a clean slate empty of pain, history, dreams.

Then I was back. Soon she began trembling, keeping her eyes on me as she moved beneath my body. I pulled all the way out and watched as she flung her hips upward to catch my cock again. It was fun and somehow new, offbeat enough that I didn't drift into that usual overwhelming feeling of familiarity.

Joy clung to me and drew her nails across my chest, again and again in the same spot until a few droplets of blood oozed free. I reached beneath, grabbed her hips and pulled her further onto me until my cock was embedded as deeply as I could go. We were rutting. I'd never truly rutted before. I'd been missing out.

She bellowed at the force of my penetration, breathing heavily but still staring directly into my eyes. She wouldn't stop watching and neither would the woman on her chest. It was enticing and unsettling, looking from one face to the other.

She climaxed again, shaking and shuddering so hard that I heard her elbows and knees crack.

"Give me more," she panted, "what's in there. Try to cut me from the inside."

"Hey!"

"You can't make me bleed but do your best." I knew in her mind she was somebody else, allowing a stranger into her.

"Holy Christ, lady, what the—?"

"Aim deep for the geek," she said, her tongue hanging out. Occasionally she seized her tattooed breast and gripped it as if she were jealous of that woman staring at us. We all had our cravings. Joy had some problems but they didn't make much of an impression on me just then. I had a man I hated inside me as well, someone my father loved and the women mooned over and who wasn't thirty pounds overweight or afraid of death. Fuck 'em both.

"Yeah, Joy, yeah," I said, feeling my climax coming on.

"Don't come yet," she ordered.

She might as well have smashed a brick across my forehead. She pulled herself off me. She rubbed her cunt juices over her nipples and into her cleavage, pressed her breasts together and shoved that other face up towards me. "Tit fuck me."

"Oh boy."

Her aureoles were crinkled now, and I gently tugged her tits apart by her nipples. I ran my cock between them and squeezed her over the shaft, her own pussy juice letting me slide easily. She held her tits together again, and I started ramming forward, with those two craving faces glaring at me.

I went slow at first, making it as sensuous as it could possibly be with the screeching speaker shrieking about extra mayo, extra ketchup, extra mustard, no ice, no pickles, no salt. You had to learn how to roll.

On each upstroke I shoved toward her mouth, letting her suck the head of my cock for an instant as she ran her tongue around it, licking the sensitive underside. I kept a steady rhythm going while loving her gorgeous tits.

"That's it," she said. I reached back and played with her clit, running two fingers around the rim of her pussy, entering her and withdrawing. She orgasmed almost immediately, and for a second, perhaps, her eyes cleared, and somehow we'd beaten back whatever had been closing in on us, step by step for most of our lives.

I murmured to her, telling her how beautiful she was, making sure that I talked to the tattoo as well.

We all have games we play deep in the well of our skulls.

I said how wonderful it felt to have her luscious breasts wrapped around my cock. I lovingly toyed with her nipples, sliding out of her cleavage and running myself over the veins of her throat, everything good and slippery, lubricated with her juice and my precum and her spit. I caressed her aureoles with my balls. You had to do something when the sweet smell of burned meat wafted past on the wind.

She gently pressed the slit of my cock open and placed the tip of one nipple into it, then the other. She orgasmed again. I moved back and forth, fucking her nipples that way for a few minutes, then slid my straining cock back into her valley. She knew I was ready to come and squeezed her breasts around me. I increased my tempo until I was groaning insanely and fucking them like a man possessed. My come started to boil up my shaft and I let her know it. I let out a deep moan and the first ribbons of come splashed against the tattoo and her neck.

"Here," she said.

I hung back exhausted while she massaged my cream into her skin, up to her neck, then into her tattoo's mouth.

Slumping forward, I came face to face with that woman she either wished she could be, or was somehow afraid of becoming, looking into those inked eyes and finding them no different from her own. The glow of sex gave Joy an extra fiery radiance that moved her from lovely to outright beautiful.

She still didn't know my name, and after that workout

the cake was looking good to me.

I dressed and crawled out of the Impala, stood outside her car peering in at her wondering what the hell was going to happen next.

I said, "You're already perfect, you don't need to wish you were somebody else."

"What do you mean?"

"Just that—"

"What kind of games did you think I was playing?"

Good question. Probably too many to count, or none at all. There was hardly ever any middle ground. Maybe I threw too much of myself into it, caught up in my own method of keeping faith with my ghosts.

She gave a nod and left it at that. The stink of grease traps blew across my face and I heard the cackle of a loudspeaker bidding welcome and people yelling more of their fatty orders into a microphone. I dressed quickly, disheveled as hell and enjoying it.

"Don't you want to know my name?" I asked her.

"Tell me the day after tomorrow," she said, climbing into the driver's seat naked. "Right here. At noon, when everybody's giving thanks in church. Fight your mediocrity, would you?"

I thought I might try. She started the Chevy and kicked it into gear, and drove away with her hand pressed over her heart as if petting the cheek of some sweaty but beloved confidante. One that held the answers to all the questions I'd never even ask.

The Scarless

MARCELLE PERKS

It was a big bed, something she could still appreciate. The plain white cotton sheet drained the heat from her exposed skin. The cameramen weren't ready yet and the longer she waited, the more the indent of her body pressed into the dampness. Yet she remained motionless, frozen to the spot. They always stressed that it was important to lie absolutely stiff, to "play dead." But they didn't want to see her soul dancing in her eyes, unlike the banal lingerie photographers who roved unfettered by their own demands and expected her to keep pace with their every turn and nuance. In cruel heels, she pranced for hours giving the camera what it wanted. Spreading her lips. Afterward, her face itched from semipermanent smile lines that took all-night crying to rinse out, to return to the doll-blank face that was her own. Until the next shoot. Here, at least, her facial expression was underexposed, an outline for a figure, or a blur. Only the body with its signature of overstretched skin connected to the powerful lens; the burning studio lights; the strange rubber domwear of the extras. Although afterward she might have to cancel studio work for weeks until the wounds faded, it gave her a numbing lull. Her body was there, but she was not. The rabbit grin that constantly fretted between her mouth and eyes would be pushed back, temporarily plumped.

Soon they would start doing it. She couldn't see or smell or touch it, but the sense of it was a tendril of shame, an idea, like a germ, she couldn't allow to get hold of her. One of the extras was unpeeling his rubber trousers, by the sound of it, to unleash what was, undoubtedly, a large dick. Without faces or skin required for the males, they could afford to harvest the biggest dicks on the circuit, from those that in other departments had fallen from grace. Underneath the rubber, the flesh was allowed to sweat unchecked, corseted to superman proportions by the ten-thousand-dollar designer suits. Domwear for the corporate analysts and Wall Street kids who could afford to have it sitting in their vast closets while they imagined wearing it. The enormous metal tripods, stationed like stranded penises, straining now, overreaching themselves. *Click, click,* a flash of light. Something was being recorded while she didn't even recognize what position she was in. And then the whispers again, the uneasy *sss sss* seemingly both near and distant, the exact meaning falling just out of reach. These masks, sometimes even without eyeholes, rendered speech muddy, the actors drowning men trying to give their names out.

Without direction of how to carry that morning's expression, she was unsure her body could live up to scrutiny when she wasn't living in it. She wanted to look good still, even if she did not. Even as an anonymous actress under the replica nineteenth-century face mask, she was becoming precious, trying to work out which way the camera was working. Did they worry about not knowing when to stop or not wanting to stop? The men were like sticky, stretchy robots, hidden in the stretched synthetic hides, being the animals they wanted to be. Two of them perhaps, working at her now, through all the inches of identity-blurring rubber. Later she would never recognize them. The squealing burn, as familiar to her as the scent of her own front room, simply stunk, the worst part about the job. Underneath the rubber, the sweat formed grooves that wobbled as they worked. But the activities of its wearers was without tangible sensation, the rubber zipped mouth dry-fucking her a burlesque of her day work, its motions insincere, dry. The guy eating her tits had no teeth now to bite them, so she didn't have to be nice to him. With rubber men, it was the shape of their bones that defined them, and the sheets beneath her that felt like flesh, the lovers she should have had. The rubber creaked and shifted. Somewhere artificial lubricant was preparing the flesh, basting it for action. The crude dull dance of their ordinary lives, displaying them as puppets without faces, working without their needing to feel something. Until they stopped trying to be lovers and became rubber men with toys.

She didn't really want to be here now that her body was reacting back into consciousness, but she didn't want to spoil it either; in fact she wanted to go down the slide, all the way to another place where everything was different. Time, rather than uselessly ticking past her, was becoming precious, every second assuming a profound significance. Uncomfortable now, she thought that she enjoyed it, but even pleasure has its doubts. Her mind wandered as the army of arrested goose bumps jumped through her skin, and the dumb pink eight-inch dildo in her pussy was forced even higher, its sound a nasal swamp beat, mud squelching under paws, prodding unkindly the prickle of the rashly shaven lips. Specially bought pan foundation evened out the red first, then got messed up, like frosted underarm sweat, under the lights. In this line on your CV they wanted to read: *perfectly symmetrical pussy, no marks or pimples.* Flesh baby-button pink. She had done it yesterday, thinking this time might be the last, before she could let the hair grow, haltingly recover. But the agent had called today to beg her to do another photo session next week. Another retro Betty Boop chic shoot, with her ebony wig and own magic shoes the color of blood, and they had requested that she turn up clean shaved. She was getting into the fetish mainstream market as well these days. So her pussy lips, shaved by her lover of yesterday, the dark-haired bi dancer from Metro's, were being mauled by their own hair follicles. Skin the color of dull veal, delicate and unwavering under the brash lights, something not meant to be exposed. Unstopped, it might begin to burst, crease into blood orange, pulped. How will they know when it really hurts? The rubber men can't really see or feel what they are doing either.

Think, think about another place. The hotel where it all began. It was elegant, like her dreams, where she auditioned for the Northern Lights Contemporary Dance group at just eighteen. Twelve years of constant training, the whittled body eager, alive. She danced just like she knew she would, passionate and controlled, a wild animal available for hire. The movements were perfect, inspired, but her body rendered it false. The instrument was wrong. They didn't like her look. Recalling it, her feet are twitching now, unhurt, unneeded, inexplicably cold. In her later life, it was the inside of her body that would be performed with, cared for. She is walking back down to her audition again and now she can feel her feet are numb, pressing into the plush red carpet of the hotel. Every step destroying something that should have formed, little flowers pulped into a mash. Her feet no longer belong to her, she does not need them. She wants her ballet shoes, to cover them up, russet like in the Michael Powell film, *The Red Shoes,* the film of her teenage dreams, but they are lost. Her nubile, trained body can no longer respond and dance. Trudging over the sumptuous, plush carpet, she probably doesn't need the shoes to leap up, she goes along the intermittent corridor, the red carpet fading, murky, the walls jumping and dancing about, breaking up, the connection in her dream uncentered. She still believes she can make it, even though once you put the shoes on you have to dance until you die. Then she stops before a surprisingly workmanlike, steel utilitarian lift. Incongruous, that such a meat cart should be waiting here in this place that crushed her dreams. They had said her hips were overly luscious, breasts too firm. Perhaps her sex jutted too conspicuously from its leotard, her nose knelt too large in her face. She was eighteen, guys called her hot, and they could tell she had been fucked. The lift was also wrong, as fake as the yuppie elevator fuck set in *Fatal Attraction* that they only used to make it easier to film the pretend penetration long shots. Now the soles of her feet are sticking to the cold floor, she can hardly lift them, her body is so heavy. Even the square resistance of the buttons against her fingers in the lift seems massive, just pressing them hurts. The lift falls, ten years on, now she knows she will never be a dancer. Now she is back here, she doesn't want to go out. Don't think now, some things have to be blocked off, forgotten about, removed from the equation. The dancer's body has been remade, laid and spread like a vestal virgin again, red on black.

She shivered furtively, using a hidden reflex. It was important to remain expressionless, body dumb, limp. On the bed she was still, consumed with waiting, holding on to the edge of a prickling, mounting pain that, if she was to let go of it for a even second, would rise up and knock her down flat. And it wasn't possible to think of why she was here, how she could be doing this. The center of meaning had moved down from the head, the capital, now it was at the pressure points that her idea of existence was scrabbling. The lights seemed to be shining more brightly now, she could feel tears trickling down her face unseen, a faint tickle that mocked, compared and contrasted, with the biting torment that the straps were inflicting elsewhere. Yes they had done it tightly, constricting the blood flow as she had requested. And something has to give.

The pressure to cry out, go purple, thrash uncontrollably, say something, was mounting as if her very anguish was affecting the rules of gravity. Normal blood flow was being circumvented and she could hear the *tick tick* panic of her pulse stiffening and bludgeoning around the restraints. The blood surfing in pointless waves in the veins of her arms and legs, bulging thickly like a painful bladder as if she had woken up with four new genitalia strategically placed. And her own vagina dilating as if it might turn itself inside out, releasing a hidden trickle of heady juice that told of her excitement in restraint; of the pleasures to come. All the colors and shapes and distances of things were changing as she lay there responding witlessly to the squeeze and pressure. This was the start of when things started losing their meanings.

She had never felt more alive and receptive. Her body seemed both heavy and light, an oxymoron she couldn't explain, the very idea of herself slipping from memory consciousness. All the little trivial afterthoughts like, was her pussy still looking fresh? had vanished. That information was not filed, not found here. You know what you can feel. In this sensitive state it was like being born again, just assuming consciousness, waking up and discovering that the whole world was one big sensory masterpiece that you had created just for that moment. Pain was an art that could never be repeated, only rehearsed, each foray a different distance, another addition to the scar tissue. Idly she wondered how long she would be able to keep up regular modeling if she kept returning here.

And the knife, when it comes, is like a little bit of love all in once piece. The tip of it, held up to the light, gleams pretty, inches seemingly into infinity. The sharp end, symbol of horror movie posters, the part that does the damage, looks so wicked and long-drawn because the idea of it hurts. And the curl and snarl of the point gleams under the eye's scrutiny. But when it is whittled over the flesh, which is expectant and boiling in its own blood, the tip feels like a kiss, a little sting of attention. Blink away the thought of it and skin really parts so easily, incredible but easy, like Moses parting the Red Sea. So when the blood comes, the seeping of it soaking into the cloth is actually a relief. A slippery soothing milk to take out the pain. We bleed so we do not need to die.

Without her clothes she has mercifully lost part of her senses. Horizontal and bound, the world didn't feel right to her, or like the way it was. It was soothing to be so disconnected, untouchable, like a faulty electric machine taken out of service. Now they were perhaps cutting her, needling the skin, cameras crunched up tight to capture every single drop of blood. The cameramen not wanting to see it, but having to do it anyway. Special footage this, not normally available. It existed for a rarefied punter who realized he had special tastes that could be pandered to, paid for. By now she could think through most of the pain, anticipate and correct for it, toy mentally with what remained. A little game, a self-imposed mind fuck for her to wrestle with, no audience. What she felt, her own currency not exchangeable. And it was the pain, and the things that it brought, not the unexpectedly good pay, that attracted and repulsed her.

A job, like any other, except that what had started off as something she couldn't even think about had become addictive, an acquired taste, a curious relief. Her body, that hunk of flesh, her life's work the controlled environment of its skin that she had spent so much time preparing this morning, was slowly being released from her care. The challenges: to get enough sun for it to glisten as a gold-textured surface, shiny, oiled, even, permanent, but never too much. Never to burn or malt. Or to get dry patches. Every day to feel just the right temperature floating in the bath, to scour every centimeter she could think of afterward with man-made bristles of a dry skin brush, savage-thoroughly, and then once again to reassure herself all of the circulation had been moved into life. Prodded. The oceans of buttermilk that have been applied, soaked-in overnight, rubbed off all over her sheets, every single piece of furniture tainted by it, reeking of decomposing grease, her body a man-made pet she can ill afford, and then all the effort, all the expense, only to wash it all off next morning, and the tedious process initiated again. Again and then again. And then the blockages, the buildup of dirty fat, slippery strings of goo, stinking fat and skin residue patties that clogged up the only orifices she relied on: the bath, the shower, the sink. The wooden floors dotted with greasy imprints, like the paws of some alien creature unaccustomed to human habits. The room deadened by the ghost of deodorants sprayed on in the past, sting of perfume catching you raw-boned in the throat, and over everything a dry residue of talcum powder, hovering, waiting to reattach itself to the skin. Even the washing machine reeling from the over-creaming, the careful measurement of the flesh, the smoothing, plucking, surfacing over the cracks.

In the straight world, without the brutal purity of pain, the women who, like Katje, were twenty-eight, youngish, were now often not young enough to face the haughty cameras; or backstage, the nubile makeup assistants, whose average age, like soldiers preparing for war, was nineteen. The irony: just as you reached the point where you had trained enough; been in enough work to have the contacts, experience; reached the point where it could start to happen, along came the first alarming gray hair, gradual dipping of the breasts, a skin change. The professionals, if they could, dated pharmacists, befriended beauticians, worked at it harder, paid for surgery when they could find it, but they expected it. It was their job, they said to everybody. Annoyed boyfriends who couldn't grip why it took them so long to get somewhere; roommates sick of seeing half-dressed neurotics at any hour, doing something to themselves, stretching, scraping, taking something out of a bottle. Nothing had been given. Not ever. They had been doing everything specially as a way of life for so long that stopping now had to be learned again. Allowed. And it had always been work. Then as children, now.

Katje thinks back to a magazine feature she once read about a model who complained that her "normal" friends didn't understand how annoying it was not to be able to eat what she wanted. It's all right for them! But the girl next door, your friends, someone off the street, got it worse. Although in the course of everyday business they could cover up most of the piece, never had to think about spots on their bumcheeks or lighten a strip of pubic flesh, just in case, nevertheless in them throbbed the dirty desire. The desire simply to be adored. Their everyday bodies ached with it just as the models, the dancers, and the actors did, the desire unchanged, but without professional motivation. For them no tax deductible allowances for anything, and mostly hardly any time to keep it up. And other big issues that stood in the way that were always more important. It was the real women who often had the feeling that these bathroom rituals could never be enough. That the minute you started rubbing yourself dry after stepping out of the bath, the skin under your breasts was already leaking sweat. That even as you stood and blow-dried the freshly wet hair, you could feel heat perspiration breaking the barrier of the clean skin. The impossibility that you could ever feel you looked the way you were wanted to look.

And so many normal women had started off as princesses. The pretty ones, those who had emitted evocative poise in their first underage competitions, whooped and danced a-go-

go, stammered posturing that was pedophiliac in all but name, metamorphosed into pressured baby flesh worked through a hundred stressed afternoons. The humbling-down local shows with filthy floors; tryouts; Proper School auditions for doll livestock; rigorous tests that began from as young as three, from as soon as the little girls could find their way to the bathroom to pee by themselves and therefore could be herded into halls, dumped in classes. Left to be prompted into positions, shouted at, stretched, blown up, cut down. By now, most of this talent have resigned themselves to their unaccomplishments with grace. Their hope folded away, but buffeted by the sense of a world where they can pay all their own bills. And this can hold them fast, give power in other means, but does not dwarf the desire. That seeps on as years tick past, unrelenting. And the women who are twenty-eight, but can no longer realize their idealized bodies, feel as keenly as a mother for a lost child the sense of missing in action, the emotional pull to recapture themselves as they were in their former picture-selves.

Uhaaaaghhhhhh. The knife is really wreaking it now, doing something bad. Right arm, top left, a contact point. She moves, tries to escape, even though they warned it would be worse if she reacted. She can imagine it now, pain blasting out raw energy, eco-power for the body system, the body's defenses springing into life even though it is mute. The body racked in nervousness. Her mind putting it into place, willing it. The glittering knife really another elaborate rubber toy, with a hidden reservoir of fake blood that the user can release with a series of mechanical clicks. The knife in the end as inconsequential as the heel of stiletto shoe, jagged edged, but destined only to skim the surface of the earth, never to force its way through. The pain real where, for what seems like hours but could be only minutes or seconds, time uncountable under the mask, the skin knits in the places it has been tied. The creases white-ringed, uncomfortable. Bondage giving always a throbbing and boiling pain. The jut of the fake blade sometimes had an edge nevertheless, even the droplets of the marketed blood, discernable, another wrench on the sensations. Katje's skin agonizing as if it were the real thing, the body's still desperation authentic somehow, even though the experience was not.

Cut to a long shot. Katje's body now arched, the legs raised, a bondage version of Marilyn Monroe in her first naked shoot. Naked, but for the mask, some rope. But still a dancer on the red sheets, unwieldy breasts thrust defiantly out from the extreme arch of the back, like a stilled limbo dancer ready to spring up, triumphantly. The hip bones rough cut, prominent. Splayed vagina as happy as a dog in mating season, its plump lips loud, one lip hanging, unconventionally lower than the other. Toby sees her pleasure is real, that the horror film mad bitch gets off on it, without telling anybody. She is too well formed to play a nubile virgin, over-muscular in parts from the various energetic training she endures to be a bimbo, but yes, she is interesting, he can use her. And he will. The punters from *Fetish Times* still get off on the fact that they can read her column as well as see her naked pictures in the same magazine. The fact that she is masked and anonymous just adding to the hype, her eclectic persona growing every month. Fans ringing with questions, other press even illegally running stills, passing it on. She remains anonymous. Someone Out There, a real person with a real job, who likes just to play a little for them.

For a moment Katje is fazed, orgasm high. It comes and goes all too quickly. She has to time it right because as soon as she's come, anything that can will chafe. Moment gone, now the comedown. The mask now sweated beyond use. The clutch of the rope at her wrists and ankles a child's game that seems sad and has gone on too long. Her bladder as usual, wanting to go. The need to satisfyingly piss, paramount. Above her, the two cameramen are talking intently about a missing light. The extras have vanished. She looks a real sight, tied up, anxiously waiting. The end bit, when all the sex acts have finished and she is herself again, is the hardest of all. Her breasts suddenly incongruous, difficult to manage without a bra. She's not really a porn actress, only allowing herself to be fucked by strangers' dildos, aping pain. Unusually shot retro bondage pics for punters who have tired of seeing it all. Who need a bit of safety, someone who won't kill them while they're getting off. As usual, the fantasy that she exists as one of those too beautiful too die. That she has to be tortured, finished off like a stray extra who wandered into a remake of *Last House on the Left*. The reality, that the dance lessons were sporadic. She had started gymnastics at fifteen, too late. That earlier she had been a dancer only in her mind, her Barbie doll had had the dresses, the dinky little shoes. And the self-conscious battle ever since to try to catch up with herself. Dancing most days, getting film extra roles, the odd fetish shoot only because she interviews the directors as a part-time journalist. That she is somehow in this world and behind it at the same time. She is everywhere and nowhere.

Now she's showered again, for the second or third time that day. Her skin is feeling too sore for another layer of body lotion. When she pissed it came with a little sting, today the guys were overzealous, but the sting-pain, though small, feels good, her body shudders deliciously at pain but she has to keep the skin undamaged for potential shoots, other work. The irony is that despite these fake gore photo shoots, she is unable, while still working as a model, to indulge in her predilections for hard CP and cutting. What was it that Brian Yunza had been told while researching skin cutting for *Return of the Living Dead, Part III?* It's not the cutting of the skin that's the problem, it's dealing with the healing process afterward.... And her skin, on the outside at least, has to look patently undamaged.

In her street clothes she becomes a different person. You would never guess. And he doesn't either. Joachim, her occasional lover, once feted horror director, now reduced to hash ravings behind closed doors, doesn't want to hurt her, physically. He indulges in mental cruelty, belittling her with tales of his actress ex-girlfriends. And of course she's not famous, yet. That's his intention, but it excites her to hear about these other women. The dark pouty one who appeared in *The Witchwoman.* I knew she would make it. Lisa, the daughter of the famous Spanish director who has now started making her own movies. Joachim litters the house with hundreds of naked photos of Lisa and thinks she suffers when he talks so raptly about his ex. That she will feel jealous, deflated by comparison. But, mmmm, the delicious decadence of it. Just thinking about Joachim's treachery, her pussy juices are warming, tingling on her freshly shaved cunt lips. And they don't even have to touch each other to get excited, it's mainly masturbatory. Mind fucking leaves no traces. She walks toward his flat, taking pink, smooth strides, but inside her mind is singing.

All McQueen's Men

ALISON TYLER

In the case of Julissa McQueen, it wasn't Humpty Dumpty but a relationship that couldn't be put back together. Perhaps it wasn't much of a relationship to start with, but Julissa had tried for so long to put up with Raymond's innumerable idiosyncracies that she wasn't ready to give up on couplehood. Not without a fight.

It turned out to be a big fight—a mean one, with Raymond cruelly claiming that she'd obviously been unfaithful to him, and Julissa storming out of the couple's penthouse apartment in tears.

"You with your goddamn poker face," he called down the hallway after her. "Finally, showing a little human emotion! Didn't know you had it in you—"

Cliché, she thought as she stalked around the block, the heels of her glossy knee-high black boots click-clacking on the pavement. *Such a fucking cliché.* He couldn't accept her fiery independence, so he chose to attack her rather than deal with his own insecurities. The thing of it was that she *hadn't* ever cheated. Not on Raymond nor any one of her previous boyfriends. The concept didn't fit her style. If a connection with a man faded, she ended the relationship before moving on to the next one.

Sure, she might have had a *thought* of cheating—but who didn't? Once or twice when an interesting specimen looked her way, she lost herself in a decadent daydream involving a satisfying situation with someone new. Perhaps while on the subway, or at the grocery store, or out on a morning run. But she'd never actually gone through with it.

Now that Raymond claimed she had—and she was fuming at the false accusation—she thought that maybe she should. Why be blamed for something, be punished for it, really, without experiencing the pleasure of actually screwing someone else?

Someone else named Blake.

And someone else named Sam.

And even someone else named Nelson.

Yes, she had them all lined up in her mind, and as she turned the corner and entered her favorite English bar, All The King's Horses, there they were, as if they'd been magically positioned, waiting for her: All McQueen's Men.

In truth, they were her poker buddies. She loved the game, had been a pro for years, but she'd never had much luck playing cards with girls. Ladies didn't seem to put as much thought into the mental war play of poker. Generally speaking, girls lost interest in their hands and started talking about clothes, or hair, or men. Julissa couldn't stand that. When *she* played cards, she wanted serious adversaries, men who had no qualms about taking her money. She wanted poker faces.

Raymond wasn't into cards. He liked playing the ponies. Or watching football on television. He didn't understand why she felt the need to join her buddies in the smoke-filled private room at the bar, where Nelson, who owned the place, had a weekly game. Raymond was invited, but after going twice, he backed out permanently. Julissa came every week. Or rather, attended every week. Mentally, she came every once in awhile when thinking about what might take place with the three studly guys who joined her at the green felt-flocked table.

Tonight was the night she'd find out.

"There she is," Blake grinned at her, motioning to the others that she'd arrived. "Let the games begin."

Julissa just smiled as she brushed a lock of midnight hair out of her startling cat-shaped eyes, and then followed the trio to the back room. Before anyone could cut the deck of cards this evening, Julissa perched herself on the edge of the table and said, "Let's raise the stakes tonight—"

Sam tilted his head at her as he waited for her to continue.

"What's on your mind?" Nelson wanted to know.

"Strip poker," Blake guessed, patting Julissa on the back with one of his large hands, touching her in an almost buddy-style that lingered just a beat too long for someone who wanted to be strictly friends.

"No," she said, shaking her head. Her long, dark hair tickled against her cheeks. "Fuck poker."

"Fuck *poker*?" Sam repeated, shocked. "What do you mean? You don't like playing with us anymore?"

"She's leaving us, boys," Blake said sadly, as if he'd always expected the day would eventually come, but had hoped against hope that it wouldn't arrive so soon.

"Not 'fuck the game,' " she quickly explained, reaching for the deck of cards and shuffling expertly. The cards danced mesmerizingly between her fingers. "But a game played for the stakes of fucking—" Another hesitation. "Fucking me, that is." One final pause, "If you're interested."

She watched the men carefully to see when they would get it. One by one, she saw the moments when they understood what she was saying—and one by one, they nodded in agreement, nodded as if they didn't care if she were pulling their chains, they definitely wanted in. Julissa herself wasn't entirely sure of what she was saying. She knew what she needed. Had thought about it enough, honestly, to have the scene entirely choreographed from start to finish. Handsome Sam would be in front of her, his faded blue jeans open, cock out, and she would lick from his balls to the tip of his shaft as Blake slid her soft skirt up to her hips and lowered her panties. Tonight, she had on a pair of pale lilac-colored ones made of lace-trimmed silk.

She wanted Nelson between her legs, fiercely lapping her pussy while Blake prepared her to receive his cock from behind, backdoor style. And by backdoor, she really meant that she wanted Blake to take her ass. Raymond wouldn't do that with her. Not that he hadn't ass-fucked a girl before, because he had and she knew it. They'd teased each other with one of those 'what have you done' conversations early on in their relationship, in the playful stage before they'd gotten serious. So yeah, she knew he'd ass-fucked a French girl in New York one summer. But he didn't do it that way with Julissa, and for some reason his refusing only made her want to go that route even more.

So she saw it all, had fantasized about it so often she felt as if she'd seen the image in a dirty movie, but that didn't mean it was going to happen. The boys had to win first, and winning wouldn't be easy. Julissa was an ace at poker. Nobody ever knew exactly what she was thinking.

"Really?" Sam asked now, and Julissa realized that her poker face was already in place. The guys truly didn't know whether or not she was putting them on.

"Really," Julissa said, dealing out the first hand.

"And Raymond?" Blake asked.

"Fuck Raymond," Julissa spat. It was clear to all of them that "fuck Raymond" was an entirely different statement from "fuck poker," and none of the men commented further. They sat down, eyeing each other carefully, and lifted their cards.

Even though she wanted this fantasy to come true more than anything else she'd ever wanted, Julissa couldn't lose on purpose. That wouldn't be right. But the guys turned out to want the evening's culmination even more than she did. For the first time ever, they created a three-man team, and they fought hard, all of them, to beat her down. Which they did. As soon as she started to lose, Julissa felt that the inevitable was happening. She couldn't draw the cards she needed, couldn't fake the boys out with any of her standard moves. Slowly, she began to accept that her fantasy was going to come true, and that made the cards shake in her hands.

"Nervous," Sam asked, reaching out to stroke her knee gently under the table.

"No," she said, folding her final hand, and she realized as she said the word that she wasn't nervous at all. She was excited, desperately wet, and ready to get started. "Let me tell you how it's going to be—"

They listened carefully to her precise instructions, and then they took their positions around her. Sam was in front, as he had to be, with his jeans splayed open, awaiting the first gentle lick of her tongue on his naked cock. He looked down at her in total awe, as she parted her full berry-glossed lips and let him in. And just as she surrounded Sam's cock with her open mouth, Nelson lowered her panties and pressed his face against her pussy.

"Oh—" Julissa murmured, her mouth full of Sam. "Oh, yes."

Blake didn't jump in right away. He watched the action for several moments before wetting his fingers and tracing them around Julissa's rear hole. He wanted her nice and wet before he plunged, and he wanted a signal from her that this was really what she needed.

Nelson continued to suckle on her clit, and Julissa, bent forward, had her mouth so full of Sam's cock that she couldn't talk at all. But she waggled her lovely ass a little, left and then right, to let Blake know that she was ready. He parted her cheeks wider and then pressed the head of his cock at her asshole. He waited a moment, and then slid in a little bit deeper. Julissa moaned ferociously around Sam's cock, and Sam picked up the pace, sliding back and forth between her lips at a rapid rhythm. Julissa couldn't get enough of him.

She swallowed forcefully, and then reached forward to cradle his balls as she continued to work him. She was driven on by the pace of Nelson between her legs and Blake fucking her smoothly from behind. Being taken back there was as exciting as she'd dreamed of. The fact that Raymond had been denying it to her so long made the pleasure even greater.

The foursome were so self-contained that not one of them heard the knock on the private door, and none noticed the intrusion until they heard a sharp intake of breath, followed by, "What the fuck is going on back here!"

Then Blake looked over his shoulder, raised his eyebrows, and simply shrugged. He was too close to coming to stop at this point. Sam didn't even bother with that much of a response, paying attention instead to the lovely Julissa, gently cradling her head as she sucked him to the root, swallowing every last drop. From his position, Nelson couldn't really see Raymond very clearly, but he knew the man was there. Being watched had always thrilled Nelson, and he put one hand on his own bulging crotch as he continued to lick Julissa's pulsing clit. He was going to come at the moment she did, and that made his entire body feel alive with impending ecstasy.

As for Julissa, when she glanced over at Raymond's face, she felt a wave of satisfaction beat through her—in the back room of All The King's Horses, and in the midst of All McQueen's Men, it was obvious that this was one relationship that would never be put back together again.

But some stories are like that—for Julissa, it didn't make her evening's ending any less happy.

About the Authors

ZACH ADDAMS is a San Francisco queer whose work has appeared in several erotic anthologies including *MASTER*, edited by N.T. Morley.

RACHEL KRAMER BUSSEL (www.rachelkramerbussel. com) serves as Senior Editor at *Penthouse Variations*. Her books include *The Lesbian Sex Book* (second edition); *Up All Night: Adventures in Lesbian Sex; Glamour Girls: Femme/ Femme Erotica; Naughty Spanking Stories from A to Z*; and *A Spanking Good Time*. Her writing has been published in over forty anthologies including *Best American Erotica 2004, Best Women's Erotica 2003* and *2004, Best Lesbian Erotica 2001* and *2004, Best Bondage Erotica*, and *Juicy Erotica*, as well in *AVN, Bust, Cleansheets, Curve, Diva, Girlfriends, On Our Backs, Oxygen, Penthouse, Playgirl*, and *The Village Voice*.

M. CHRISTIAN is the author of *Dirty Words* and *Speaking Parts*. He is the editor of *The Burning Pen, Guilty Pleasures*, the *Best S/M Erotica* series, *The Mammoth Book of Tales of the Road*, and *The Mammoth Book of Future Cops* (with Maxim

Jakubowksi). His short fiction has appeared in over 150 books including *Best American Erotica, Best Gay Erotica, Best Lesbian Erotica, Best Transgendered Erotica, Best Fetish Erotica*, and *Best Bondage Erotica*. He lives in San Francisco.

DANTE DAVIDSON is the pseudonym of a professor who teaches in Santa Barbara, California. His short stories have appeared in *Bondage, Naughty Stories from A to Z*, and *Sweet Life 1* and 2. With Alison Tyler, he is the coauthor of *Bondage on a Budget* and *Secrets for Great Sex After Fifty*. Currently on sabbatical, he is living in Rome.

REBECCA HENDERSON has published poetry, short stories, essays, and travel stories. She works full-time in public relations, takes classes sporadically, writes obsessively, and adores her three children. She lives in St. Louis, Missouri.

MICHELLE HOUSTON (www.eroticpen.net) is a member of the Erotica Readers and Writers Association and the author of the e-books *Bedtime Tales, Bi Sexual*, and *Naughty Whispers*.

MARILYN JAYE LEWIS is the founder of the Erotic Authors Association. Her erotic short stories and novellas have been widely anthologized in the United States and Europe. She is the author of the erotic romance novels *When Hearts Collide, In the Secret Hours*, and *When the Night Stood Still*. Her forthcoming books include *Lust* (the complete collection of her short erotic fiction), the novels *Twilight of the Immortal* and *Greetings from the Dream Factory*, and *Freak Parade*, a memoir.

JULIA MOORE is the co-author of *The Other Rules: Never Wear Panties on a First Date and Other Tips*. Her short stories have appeared in *Sweet Life 1* and *2; Naughty Stories from A to Z, 1* and *2; Batteries Not Included*; and on the website www.goodvibes.com.

N.T. MORLEY has published more than a dozen novels of erotic dominance and submission, including *The Parlor, The Limousine, The Circle, The Visitor,* and the trilogy *The Library, The Castle,* and *The Office*. Morley is the editor of the double anthology *MASTER/slave*.

DAWN M. PARES is a graduate of the University of Central Florida Honors Program, and holds a BA in Creative Writing. She has been the editor of an independent weekly newspaper and a copywriter for an ad agency. She currently lives in Orlando, Florida, and is working on a novel.

EMILIE PARIS is a writer and editor. Her first novel, *Valentine*, is available on audiotape from Passion Press, for whom she also abridged the seventh-century novel *The Carnal Prayer Mat*. Her short stories have also appeared in *Naughty Stories from A to Z, Sweet Life 1* and *2*, and on the website www.goodvibes.com.

An avid horror film fan, **MARCELLE PERKS** has written for a range of horror and film publications, including *The BFI Companion to Horror, British Horror Cinema, Gothic Lifestyle, Gay Times, Fangoria, Kamera,* and *The Guardian*. Her erotic writing has previously appeared in *Sex Macabre* and *Tales from the Clit*. She also danced as a naked extra in the horror film,

Faust: Love of the Damned (2000) and did dialogue work on the Danish erotic film, *All About Anna.*

TOM PICCIRILLI (www.tompiccirilli.com) is the author of a dozen novels including *A Choir of Ill Children, November Mourns, The Night Class,* and *Coffin Blues.* He's published over 150 stories in the horror, fantasy, mystery, and erotica genres. He's also been a World Fantasy Award finalist and is a three-time Bram Stoker Award-winner.

THOMAS S. ROCHE's short stories have appeared in a wide variety of magazines, websites, and anthologies, including the *Best American Erotica* series, the *Best Gay Erotica* series, and the *Best New Erotica* series. His own books include the *Noirotica* series of erotic crime-noir anthologies, the forthcoming *Naughty Detective Stories from A to Z,* and *His* and *Hers,* two collections of erotica he co-wrote with Alison Tyler. He recently began taking erotic photographs, and showcases both his writing and his photography at www.skidroche.com.

HELENA SETTIMANA lives an otherwise uneventful life in Toronto, Canada, where she wears funny hats and teaches pottery to women and men exercising *Ghost* fantasies. Her short fiction, poetry, and essays have appeared on the Web at www.erotica-readers.com, www.scarletletters.com, and www.cleansheets.com. In print, her work has been featured in *Erotic Travel Tales*; *Best Women's Erotica 2001, 2002,* and *2004*; *Penthouse*; *Best Bondage Erotica*; *The Mammoth Book of Best New Erotica*; *Hot and Bothered 4*; and many others. In addition to moonlighting as Features Editor at the Erotica Readers and

Writers Association she is busy assembling her first collection of short fiction, and there is a novel in the works.

A. J. STONE was born and raised in New York City. A feature film producer, she currently resides in Los Angeles. This is her first published erotic short piece.

SASKIA WALKER (www.saskiawalker.co.uk) is the author of an erotica novel, *Along for the Ride*. Her work appears in *Seductions: Tales of Erotic Persuasion*, *Sugar and Spice*, *More Wicked Words* and *Wicked Words 5* and *8*, *Naughty Stories from A to Z 3*, *Naked Erotica*, *Taboo: Forbidden Fantasies For Couples*, and *Sextopia*

ERIC WILLIAMS has published erotica in *Sweet Life* and *Naughty Stories from A to Z 3*. He is fixated on the concept of threesomes, for better or worse.

About the Editor

Alison Tyler is a shy girl with a truly dirty mind. Over the past ten years, she has written more than twenty naughty novels including *Learning to Love It, Strictly Confidential, Sweet Thing, Sticky Fingers,* and *Something about Workmen* (all published by Black Lace). Her novels have been translated into Japanese, Dutch, German, and Spanish. Her stories have appeared in *Sweet Life 1* and *2; Erotic Travel Tales 1* and *2; Best Women's Erotica 2002, 2003,* and *2005; Best Fetish Erotica; Best Lesbian Erotica 1996;* and *Taboo* (all published by Cleis Press); and in *Wicked Words 4, 5, 6, 8,* and *10;* and *Best of Black Lace 2* (Black Lace); *Best S/M Erotica* and *Noirotica 3* (Black Books); *Sex Toy Tales* (Down There Press); and *Mammoth Book of Best New Erotica* (Carroll & Graf).

With long-time writing partner Dante Davidson, she is the co-author of *Bondage on a Budget* (Pretty Things Press), and she edited *Down & Dirty 1* and *2; Juicy Erotica; Naked Erotica;* and *Naughty Stories from A to Z 1, 2,* and *3* (all Pretty Things Press); *Batteries Not Included* (Diva); *Heat Wave* and *Best Bondage Erotica* (both Cleis Press). With Thomas Roche, she is the co-author of *His* and *Hers,* two collections from Pretty Things Press (www.prettythingspress.com).

Ms. Tyler believes that when playing with multiple partners, it's safest to refer to everyone as "darling."